Bernie Unrau DDS

CalTex Press

PO Box 69014
162 Ave S.W.
Calgary AB T2Y4S0
www.caltexpress.com

Rising by Dr Bernie Unrau copyright c 2009
c2010. All rights reserved. Book design c 2010
by Cal Tex Press.

Published by Cal Tex Press
#3413 16320 24St SW
Calgary AB T2Y5A1
403-246-0523
www.caltexpress.com

No part of this publication may be reproduced,
stored in a retrieval system or transmitted in any
way by any means electronic, mechanical,
photocopy, recording or otherwise without the
permission of the author except as permitted by
Canadian /US/International copyright law. This
novel is a work of fiction. Names, descriptions,
entities and incidents included in the story are
products of the author's imagination. Any
resemblance to actual persons, events and entities
is entirely coincidental.

ISBN: 978-0-9784552-7-9

Printed in the United States
Publishers' Graphics
140 Della Court
Carol Stream Il. 60188
888-404-3769
www.pubgraphics.com

RISING c2009 c2010

1) Rise
2) Omen
3) Unwrapped
4) Seasons
5) Culinary Delight
6) Cabin Fever
7) Chiller
8) Diving
9) Discovery
10) Angels and Demons
11) Last Resort
12) Trails
13) Smoke Signals

PROLOGUE

In a pristine picturesque setting at the end of the road in a remote region of a dense deciduous forest lies a hotel. The Prominence O' Way, a gracefully aging rustic structure, sits atop a desolate mesa dating back to former royalty. The POW has opened it's doors to a variety of distinguished guests….yet, the idyllic inspirational setting is not without it's share of tragedies….4 ghosts are rumored to reside within it's hallowed halls … two of which were former staff, driven to suicide by sinister forces…..an anonymous guest, the ghost of 'Honest Abe' (aka Abraham Lincoln) peacefully puffing on a carved peace pipe. The intoxicating aroma lingering in the lofty lobby greets you…the bottles rattling from the back of the bar, with it's commanding, breathtaking view of the lake lost in the distance. The 4th ghost, the wife of the former chef who vanished mysteriously decades ago….., the victim of foul play, or some thing much more sinister? Possessed by an evil ever recurring spirit? Intent on wreaking havoc upon all who enter the hotel's hallowed halls? The town of Wutherington, meaning loud blowing wind, is nestled in it's unique nook and cranny alongside Enchanted Bay. The sleepy resort slips into gentle slumber and hibernation for most of the year intent on passing away peacefully far removed from the rat race of the rest of the world. What an idyllic inspirational spot for an upcoming wordsmith, a dedicated dentist turned novelist and aspiring screenwriter to pass away the winter months accompanied only by his trusty typewriter and enchanting young bride. The couple are about to experience a shocking surprise and abrupt end to their picture perfect private honeymoon in the majestic albeit mysterious recesses of the hotel. A horrific unexplained haunting nightmare the likes of which they could have never imagined.

1: Rise

> "Though my soul may set in
> darkness, It will rise in perfect
> light, I have loved the stars too
> fondly to be fearful of the night.'
> - Sarah Williams

One is overcome by the solitary lone sentinel towering high above the surrounding pristine panorama. A harbinger of hope, a beacon of light, amongst a deep dark green carpet of deciduous forest....like a misplaced lighthouse guiding many a weary wanderer to it's gates. The rustic aging rickety structure rises prominently above the point as if beckoning those who dare to enter the

enchanting, effervescent town of Wutherington
from the Old Yorkshire English meaning loud
blowing winds; nestled in it's own nook and
cranny, it's little niche, lost in time….just below
the guardian of the gates, the POW Prominence
O'Way . Upon passing into the narrow gulley to
the town's oldest structure, the Killroy Lodge
snuggled up against Enchanted Bay…the POW is
ever present in the corner of your eye….as if
watching, waiting ….for it's next unsuspecting
guest to arrive.

   Dr Gum knew the isolated area well…the
International Peace Park at land's end so to speak,
the end of the road…the 'last stop'…set in the
serene rugged wilderness…a place to get away
from it all…to reenergize, recuperate and restore a
sense of sanity in this sordid hell bent for leather
pace we are all accustomed to….or so he thought.

   His young new wife, Roxy, was eager to
accompany him, aroused by the lure, like a
clandestine romantic tryst in the dense north
American …To truly become one with nature and
explore each other …afresh, to renew the sacred
marriage vows and delve deeply into the inner self,

the unexplored soul. For he was granted special privileges bestowed only upon a select few, including the former royalty, who had the foresight to envision an enchanting villa at the edge of the known universe…at the time. The harsh weather and unpredictable sudden storms kept the tourist season to a minimum of two, at best four months. At the culmination of a busy season, the structures were slapped with signs, boarded up and the sleepy town of Wutherington once again sank into a deep slumber …satisfied to settle into a long winter's nap and dormancy….awaiting the spring thaw runoff to refresh the depleted stores… the rise of the first spring bud sprouting from the cold rocky ground…..The dedicated dentist turned novelist and screenwriter's reservations granted an entire 'off season' in which to languish and lap up the luxurious albeit dated accommodations, conduct his research, hone his penmanship, carry on in the enchanted stately manor…feasting on everything the former regal getaway had to offer. Sip up the inspiring sights and sounds of the austere abode …his passing season….

And so it was for our two adventurers…about

to embark upon the short and sweet desperately needed interlude…

The ludicrous lewd intervention would forever disrupt their deepest trust in one another… redefining everything they held close and dear. For logic and sound reasoning seemed to play no part in the mind shattering experience they encountered in the hallowed halls of the haunted hotel that year, 33 years to the day, the 'Overlook' Hotel in 'The Shining' nearly trapped the writer and inhabitants for all eternity in it's hideous haunting grip.

The late model Lexus idled, lingering on the road…the GPS.. gave no distinct fixed address …the signal simply disappeared…slipped under the radar at land's end… or so it seemed. It gave the two a glimpse of the grand aging gargantuan Gateway to the Rockies….Dr Gum tapped the screen on the sophisticated sensory illuminated console….several times.

"Damn it!"

"Lost again are we?" asked his curious companion, and young wife. The soft complexion of her face had a cutesy girlish glow to it…in the receding hours of daylight like the lingering side effects of a romantic energetic interlude, an afternoon of delightful and lusty lovemaking.... "There's only one way in and out of that hotel...".

"Need I be reminded" the ornery perfectionist, and stickler for detail had neglected to consider a plan B...they were here for a good time..and potentially a long time, weather permitting. The thought of passing the time in the provocative historic hotel seemed to exude a sensual response from his perky wife...She'd finally have him all to herself to do as she pleased ....unfettered, free from distractions of the former dental practice slowly transitioning into a thriving publishing, screenwriting production house...mind you the mountains of paperwork accumulated at the same speed of thought pace... in lieu of the monotonous mundane medical dental histories...the last minute 'no shows'... the absent apparitions of former smiling faces ....the charts... were now cleverly crafted million dollar concepts ....she recalled how he constantly reminded her,

"Imagination is infinitely more important than knowledge" according to another prolific professional….albeit Albert Einstein depleted the department stores of chalk rather than rapid rolling ball point pens.

She was the 'meaning and inspiration' in his life…the amusing muse…. and that "nothing shall ever come between them…" A cool chilly breeze abruptly stirred her from her dreamy state as if in a post coital recoil as she rolled down the window merely a crack….

"It's going to be a mean one, an early winter" he stated prognostically…never placing more than a penny in a poker game that was dependent upon predicting the outcome of the dramatic daily temperature fluctuations. Betting on an inhibited filly at the track was a surer thing.

He activated the temperature controlled heating system. It too belched out a blast of icy air that nipped at his nubile nymph's leggings….

"If you don't know where you're going, any road will get you there." (Lewis Caroll) "Did we miss the turnoff?

"To travel hopefully is a better thing than to arrive." (Robert Louis Stevenson) he debated with himself, having second thoughts about bringing her along?

The solitary sentinel, like a lone watchdog appeared slowly over the last rise in the road, deceptively ascending as they gained altitude. A chill went up Roxy's spine, reverberating to her very bone. She shuddered shocked by the cold breeze or equally chilling structure....she didn't know what came over her.

"Ah, here we are....." he announced joyfully. Not a soul in sight, he cautiously took the narrow turnoff at the bottom of the hill....then snaked his way up the sinuous pathway to the summit....

The imposing old structure seemed out of place and time with it's rectilinear lines set against the rugged rough sharply gutted backdrop....the large parking lot...like a large landing pad for the gods....or tee off for the jolly green giant...atop the massive mesa that tapered and dropped off dramatically to the lake below....was vacant. The Lexus inched toward the entrance; a small ornate opening adorned with a crown and 3 ostrich feathers,....symbolic of faith and contemplation ...oft depicted with keys or a horseshoe in it's mouth. The meat of the bird lean, high in calcium and iron.

   Dr Gum peered across the picture perfect panorama. In the foreground he noticed the rows of overturned soil like a massive vegetable garden off the edge of the imposing impediment, a highly manicured waist high hedge…Odd, he thought to himself…such a short growing season…only the hardiest of plants…potatoes perhaps? rhubarb.. Too barren and breezy for tomatoes…

   He parked the vehicle…Roxy slowly stepped out to inhale the heavenly fragrance…a blend of alpine grasses and dense deciduous forest…she became dizzy from the intoxicating, tempting tree bark and tall grasses gushing in her lungs, her tidal volume overwhelmed as her husband stepped to the back of the automobile to grab a mountain of luggage… Must've packed at least 27 dresses he estimated. Intent on parading around the palace in all her glory…all dressed up and no place to go…the gala events, the glitz and glamour…the three fun filled months of festivities had come and gone with the wind….Yet, he figured she packed for halloween, Christmas and a festive new year's eve in the event they'd linger that long…

"How dee doo?" the words echoed over the gusty mesa....A muscular middle aged man of native American descent, a blend of Blackfoot, indigenous to the area emerged suddenly...A large grin spanned his sweaty, sooty face. He tossed the shovel aside...in deep thought, slowly mulling something through his mind... "Dr Rum is it?"

"It's Gum, and this is my wife Roxy." His firm albeit deceptively delicate handshake tipped him off that he was probably moonlighting as a maintenance man to supplement his income as he oft did during his formative years of medical training. A native medicine man perhaps?

"I'm Running Deer." A cliché? albeit catchy... name...no cause for concern...especially since the one man show seemed to keep the place running! "Here let me get those!" then swiftly hoisted the heavy luggage from the trunk and carried them to the front door. He set them down delicately. The aging detailed features creaked and groaned as he negotiated the keys into the custom crafted locks reminiscent of a monstrous medieval castle, a precautionary measure to keep the paranormal activists and ghost hunters out!. For years local spirit seekers and amateur camera crews were caught camping out in the hotel by local park wardens…The door creaked and moaned defiantly as it slowly crept ajar. Like an eerie early warning signal intent on informing the occupants of an intruder…One was immediately captivated by the lofty lobby and large floor to ceiling panes on the opposite expanse permitting a breathtaking panorama of the entire deeply carved mountainous lake valley lost in the distance.

"Honey I'm home!"…In lieu of carrying his wife over the threshold, as she stood there tapping her designer footwear in disgust, he marveled at the monumental size of the foyer…Looking up into the lofty space…several foreboding rings of steel, massive 'wagon wheel' chandeliers with countless candelabras in small glass boxes tapered like a layered wedding cake to the ceiling. A small square recess, a secret 'trapdoor' visible only to the discerning eye sat squarely at the gradually tapering tiered balconied space. The infamous aperture, where several staff had suffered a fatal fall. Either mangled on the menacing tangled web of the chandelier which wrapped itself around the lobby or striking the dusty hardwood floor below. Either method, an end to the utter madness they had endured…smitten by the hotel manager or as some locals suggested, a sinister spirit which lay embedded in the very walls of the rickety old structure….

"Why don't you relax, have a look around? I'll take these up to your room." Running Deer disappeared into a cleverly crafted metal cage, an elevator set off near the main front doors, opposite a grand staircase that seemed carved right out of the intricate woodwork…The rickety mechanism echoed throughout the empty foyer…as it found it's way up to the 4th floor. The world's slowest elevator? And why only part way?…He negotiated the larger hallway ever peering up at the next floor. He decided not to place the couple in 512, the 'haunted room'.. not wanting to spoil their 'honeymoon'. No one requested the room, unless the hotel was entirely booked during the regular season. No point in putting them in harm's way he figured. They'd find out what was in store… soon.

He set their luggage in one of the large 'Lakeview' Suites…home to legendary leaders, royalty, presidents, prominent entertainment personalities and those who simply sought to get away from the cares of the world, in style. The austere space still oozed simple sumptuous cozy creature comfort. Sparsely appointed, the room had a fanciful grained rosewood trim, a few Victorian aged dressers and drawers..a high back comfy sofa and chairs, end tables each with tiffany lamps and a small radio. He placed the Samsonite luggage on the large king sized bed…then opened the ensuite door to reveal a deep European style tub and wrap around shower.

Roxy was aroused by the opulent, ornate and certainly out of the way locale. A perfect choice to renew their faith, and their first chance to truly get away. Her nervousness showed.

"It's sooo beautiful. Just what the doctor ordered. It's the perfect place to get away from it all. To write that novel you've been dying to pen. I'm so glad you asked me to tag along." She rushed toward him. He turned, wasting no time to reciprocate with a big bear hug in the middle of the massive meeting space. "I love you sweet heart." He eyed the upper balconies…as if expecting approval or applause from the ghosts of former star studded celebrities. Amongst all the glamorous guests who had looked out eyeing the who's who of distinguished guests to grace the gala gathering place....A little performance anxiety perhaps? Sharing the same feelings even presidents must've felt, taking the plunge with their first ladies in waiting. Hopefully he'd rise to the occasion this evening, their first night in their new, anything but humble, abode. His mistress still in his arms, he spun her around for a 360 degree panorama picking out the perfect spot from which to pen his book.

"This is it!" He released her from his grip and stepped toward the edge of the sparsely appointed lobby. Several clusters of finely threaded leather covered sofas and chairs were strategically arranged to allow the most compelling views of the lake. The small enclaves were maximized for optimum privacy amidst the exceptional acoustics of the chamber. The massive ebony desk, more massive than the remnants of the Resolute in the Oval office struck his attention immediately. The perfect place and strategic vantage point from

which to write his most promising best seller.
He took his place behind the desk ceremoniously.
One eye ever present on the endless array of fine
whiskies and other enticing intoxicants lining the
glass shelves of the Weeping Willow lounge to his
right. Brandy snifters, long Cuban cigars, it's
tobacco leaves rolled on the thighs of virgins. To
while away the long cold creative nights; of course
he had his trusty loving companion to keep him
company under the covers of the night…With one
sweeping glance he imagined the former glitz and
glamour of the Hotel in it's great Gatsby hey day.
Great Neck, N.Y. during the jazz era, the boot
legging prohibition, running whiskey across the
border. The Great Northern Railway, the effort of
the determined 'Empire Builder' James J. Hill; a
tireless tycoon who turned the dream into a reality
during the midst of the depression. Where all other
rails had gone bankrupt, his line stood the test of
time and slowly reached fruition with the erection
of 7 massive monuments, the Glacier Park Hotels
in the NE USA. Inspite of early set backs, blinded
in one eye by an arrow accident, JJ blazed a trail
through the harsh wilderness. He subdued every

obstacle…including the native Indian population with a little help from President Grover Cleveland, who later repealed laws permitting Hill to run track through treacherous Blackfoot Indian territory.

A noise jilted him back to reality…the irritable trapdoor….. began to take it's toll. It slammed suddenly as a gust of wind rose over the bluff …literally shaking the structure, creaking and groaning in an eerie defiance, determined to remain rooted atop the desolate mesa for the remainder for the century…for all eternity for that matter.

Running Deer returned from his seemingly endless run up and down the perpetual motion machination, practically at a standstill. The cumbersome stairs may have been a quicker alternative.

"There's an ample supply for winter" remarked the connoisseur of alcoholic concoctions. Roxy turned toward him admiring the breathtaking view from the front window. Her demeanor changed drastically as her eyes darted around the Weeping Willow lounge. She realized her worst fear, the lurking demons, that had haunted their marriage…

She hoped to bury the past…former fiascos of her own family linked to the liquor…She had tried to lock them away in the recesses of her mind. Not fan or fuel the flames of desire, the lurid lust and endless legacy of carnage. She could not fathom the endless array of enticing colorful sparkling glass; it unsettled her. It sent a shock wave through her…which seemed to reverberate through the very shelves…did she imagine it or about to realize her worst fear?

"Why don't we run into town…grab a few things before the general store shuts down?" he paused, then added "I have a surprise."

Dr Gum reached out and took Roxy by the arm, she still in a state of shock.. He assumed the ambience; the awe inspiring view, and the altitude.

Running Deer turned off the porch lights, to conserve energy perhaps? His jalopy was parked outside, an old Ford truck that merely had to get him from point A to B…and the occasional run to the nearest town of Buffalo Butte in the event of an unforeseen life threatening emergency.

Dr Gum couldn't get over the lumpy lines of overturned soil and sod…perhaps a Blackfoot ceremony, but he lost his gumption to ask RD, captivated by the awesome sight and silence of the remote retreat. Roxy too, was lost in the moment, deep in thought, inspired by the tranquil treed terrain. RD looked to his left then turned abruptly onto the two lane highway as if by instinct. No one ever came down the isolated road this time of year anyway. Only those heading out of town! The Ford crept along…to the left, the narrow inlet know as Enchanted Bay separated the hilltop from the town of Wutherington. A row of rustic cabins and tall pine trees lined the lake on the town's side. RD didn't bother to signal as he negotiated the sharp corner… onto main street. A lone innkeeper was climbing his stepladder affixing a shingle to his establishment. K.I..L.L..R..O..then a marked gap…then the remaining Y…Why the gap? Like a game of hangman wondered the astute dentist rather amused yet equally alarmed by the odd name…of the lodge. The Killroy? He had read the original structure built, even before the POW hotel circa 1927, had mysteriously burnt to the ground the previous year. Some sordid rumors suggested spontaneous combustion. The maids doing the

dirty laundry, the lakeside lodge's little secret?
Rumors circulated. Yet later dispelled, the cause of
the blaze due to careless handling of laundry
cleaners? Some local folk still claim there's more
to it than meets the eye. That the poor maid was
not to blame. He decided to let sleeping dogs lie
and delve into it deeper another day.

The Ford ambled down the deathly still main
street. It seemed to slip into slumber as they passed
the old mortician's cabin, Jebb Evans. His daughter
Becky, the brunt of several jokes he had read some
where; 'that she'd buried more stiffs than he did'!

"A real ghost town!" remarked RD…as they
passed the last pine tree. A long finger reached out
into the lake. A lone fixture sat at the end of the
dock fixing some fishing line or mending a frayed
knot. No one paid particularly much attention. First
and foremost was the foreboding presence of the
POW Hotel as if perched atop it's regal throne
towering over it's loyal subjects, the captive
audience enclosed in the steep walls of the valley.
Carved over eons of time..the small spit of land, a
stone's throw from the ever present POW. Always
within gun sight; watching from every possible

vantage point, escape impossible. The Ford pulled into the parking lot of the Lakeview Inn. An adjoining grocery store supplied all the rations for the rest of the town throughout the summer.

The three trekked into the store as if lost, out of time and place. The store keeper was shutting everything down.. they'd arrived just in the nick of time it seemed.

"She's gonna be a long cold one.. felt a chill to my very bone."

"We'll just grab a few things Gus.." assured RD then they'd be out of his hair.

"Help yourselves, I'm headin' for the hills, Beverley Hills. Anywhere but this God forsaken ice box. Why wait for spring?" he chuckled.

They cleared him out of house and home, and quickly emptied the shelves.

"Plannin' to feed an army…of ghosts?" he asked facetiously. RD rushed them out the door before the comment sunk in. They placed the goods in the back of the truck . He turned down toward the dock. The forlorn long faced fisherman wearing an old grimy baseball cap with the lone word, and presumptuous title - 'Captain' emblazoned on it.

"You folks need a lift?"

The three adventurers looked at each other.

"Well, you're in luck. There's always room for one more."

He got off his stool and stepped up to the plank, a long rickety old board spanning the gap between them and the Miss Wutherington. An imposing 100 passenger double decker craft…the only vessel still out on the lake…about to be tucked in for winter.

"Surprise!" announced RD.

"Watch your step" warned the captain raspingly. They trek across the rickety gang plank…peering nervously into the deep dark icy waters. Roxy rushed to the upper deck, cautiously gripping the icy aluminum handrail for a better bird's eye view off the bow. As she turned around the presence of the POW unnerved her. It's appearance, akin to an angry relative or ancestor; the large lobby windows like two temperamental eyelets…peering over a fence? Both curious about who's coming to town, cunning, conniving; not sure if it wanted to be bothered by company! But that was only her interpretation of the image. The captain introduced himself as Rick and quickly took the wheel of the vessel. Dr Gum joined Roxy up top. He knew the fresh air would do them a world of good. Three loud blasts startled them…as the seasoned mariner maneuvered the massive marine marvel slowly from her moorings. As if gently easing a sword from it's scabbard, the old scalawag backed the behemoth from it's narrow berth. He cranked the wheel hard and spun her on a dime…then beelined for the bell tower high atop the POW.

"Off to the left at the bottom of Enchanted Bay" blared the intercom…breaking the peace and quiet they so desperately longed for.. "lies the wreck of the Germaine in some 20-60' of water. An old rum runner… that ran out of luck."

The vessel careened close to the rocky shore below the crumbling cliffs of the hotel.

"Several sea otters crashed up on the rocks attempting to land in the middle of winter." They got the picture... menacing, extremely isolated in the dead of winter. No way in or out.

The vessel picked up speed at the head of the lake…beelining for a point on the opposite shore, she kicked up quite a wake. Dr Gum and Roxy hustled below deck out of the fierce frisky icy

breeze. They ventured to the stern looking back
in amazement and angst…at the town receding in
the distance. Only the POW seemed to remain in
suspended animation, surreal, staring back …
…..hypnotizing them.

"Ah to be in love…again" lauded the captain as
he eyed the two lovebirds in the large rear view
mirror. Roxy was still spellbound by the structure
as Dr Gum realized the captain was approaching a
deserted beach at breakneck speed.. Was he drunk?
Fell asleep at the wheel? he wondered?…In one
swift motion the learned laker lassoed a small
post…as if entered in the One hundred thousand
dollar rodeo finals at the Calgary Stampede. The
massive vessel ceded to the small frayed rope and
came to an abrupt stop inches from the shore. They
hopped off at the small stony beach, Crypt Lake
trail head. RD rushed to start a fire, grabbing
prepared kindling from his previous outing. The
soothing warmth was most welcome by one and
all. The crackling embers leapt into the air like
excited fireflies…Roxy watched them rise amongst
the tips of the tall pine trees lost in the twilight
zone. Her attention always veered to the ominous

ever present oppressive dark outline dotting the opposite end of the lake. She swore she saw a light come on.

"They're at it again" announced RD accustomed to the routine ritual.

"Not another 'tale from the crypt'?" chuckled Rick, an insider quip?

"No point spookin' 'em albeit the locals know". Roxy and her husband looked at each other perplexed. "A vision?.. There was a wise man and woman who ascended to the top of Chaff Mt, Along the way he killed a porcupine, used the blood to color the garment bright red. They were the prettiest couple. As many a young brave embarks on a 'vision quest'…to the top of the Mt. to remain for three days from sunrise til sunset… with only his 'medicine bundle'; sleeping on only buffalo skulls as pillows awaiting his 'vision' to determine his destiny…."

"It's dead" as Roxy tried her phone…no link to the outside world.

"Won't get any reception 'round here, it's a dead zone" commented Captain Rick.

Their anxious faces radiated in the glowing

crackling fire.

"I see a sick elk" says RD somberly, disturbed. Normally a sign of health, this was a bad omen. Equally frightening was a furry white rabbit, a death omen in Blackfoot lore, not the lucky rabbit's foot.

"We have to go back to the POW at once to smoke a pipe," the only known remedy. "But first, a 'ghost dance'!" Roxy and Dr Gum were moved by the clever charade, curious, caught unawares, drawn deeper into the unfolding drama....as RD shuffled around the fire chanting....

"Claims to make him practically bulletproof.. impervious to pain" comments the Captain.

"It is done." RD had deliberated, in a desperate attempt to avert something....

They returned to the vessel, let the cinders of the smoldering fire rise......then beelined back to Wutherington. At the other end of the lake at Ghost Haunt, a couple of park wardens thought nothing of the rising smoke...the tell tale last sign of the end of the season and the advent of a long cold harsh winter. They kept an eye on it...though.

The bow light pierced the darkness that crept

over the lake, for but a short distance. Roxy was fixated on an upper story light...Dr Gum, too, became entranced in the odd exception to the rule. The ruler's left the lights on? They bid the Captain goodbye, likely the last they'd see of him 'til spring. They left the parking lot, the prominent beacon on the hill guiding the way.

RD couldn't recall leaving any lights on....He then realized this season would be no different from all the rest. Up to it's old tricks...teasing, taunting, terrorizing the endless list of travelers who had attempted to stay for the duration of the winter. The irritable rambunctious rabble rouser remained, the entity would likely outlive even him; it'd certainly outlived his welcome!

2: Omen

"Writers really live in their mind
and the hotels of the soul."
- Edna O'Brien

The ghostly silhouette of the structure stood out against the starry backdrop as they neared the front entrance. The strange solitary beacon, an upper floor light in a corner window, brought them home. RD slowly inserted the master key in the lock, then pushed the heavy oak door open.

"Lights on, nobody's home, huh?" stated Dr Gum on edge as he peered through the empty expanse to the large panes projecting the faint moonlight into the interior of the lobby. The furniture seemed to take on a life of it's own. The ghostly high back silhouettes as if assembled, mingling in a stately function already in progress, beckoned them inside. Roxy remained immobile, her imagination running away with her. Spirits of days gone by seemed to brush up against her...but deep down she knew it was only the icy gust coming in from the front door which suddenly slammed shut.

RD flicked the light switch, bathing the lobby in brilliant candle light from atop the multi tiered cake like chandelier all the way to the top of the 7 story space. It cast several sinister shadows into the upper balconies and entryways. RD traversed the foyer through the Stallworthy Dining Room, the chairs and tables were covered in white sheets as if awaiting a large banquet of well heeled socialites, into the colossal culinary center. Many a seasoned chef wielding a razor sharp cleaver had chopped, sliced and diced an exquisite esophageal extravaganza. Roxy followed her husband at her own risk. As she reached the large arched entry way she was overcome by a chill, a 'vision', a premonition as she peered around at the endless stack of unopened boxes, and crates of food? Presumably they'd be rotting by now yet no putrid lingering odors originated from the card board containers. RD attempted to start the large ranch style stoves and several of the grills…Roxy continued to scope the large experimental eating space. A loud whoosh startled them as the stove burners finally ignited….he searched the shelves for a large metal pot in which to place some water. While they waited for it to boil, he ushered them through the Stallworthy Dining Room… the Valley View Tea Room to the right with a view to die for, over the entire sculpted glacial gulley and lake, sat dormant in disuse since the last lady Diana tribute.

As they ventured across the lofty space….the creaky structure continued to moan and groan seemingly like a giant stirred from it's sleep. The relentless howling winds crawled up the hill carrying a fine mist from the water's surface. The occasional upper floor window or door, shifted by the continuous surge of the structure over the years, slammed shut.

"Do you smell that?" Roxy was amazed, she

wasn't wearing any perfume, her natural scent certainly could've aroused the savage beast. As they took small short sips of air through their nasal passageways, a distinct aromatic tobacco fragrance indeed was present. A cigar or pipe? A definitive, strong odor of a peace pipe perhaps? The couple was stunned.

"It's honest Abe" chuckled RD familiar with the recurring clairalience..from the French clair - clear and alience - smelling. An extrasensory form of perception in parapsychology, referring to the sense of smell. RD flicked the switches into the Weeping Willow Lounge. They took a long look around.

"There's no one here."

"Saved me a light" chuckled RD....as he reached behind the bar....slowly producing a pipe in an ashtray and a pack of large native tarot cards. RD's remedy for the ill elk vision quest omen apparently appeased.

"Second hand smoke can kill you" warned Dr Gum prophetically. Roxy wasn't so sure about remaining in the lounge. The liquor bottles kept her in a trance like state, a continuous cascading kaleidoscopic effect as she sauntered along the long alabaster marble surface of the ornate oak bar....

"What was your vision? And what did you mean, they're at it again?" she began to probe, out of the blue.

RD was reluctant to reveal any details directly to them, fearing they'd refrain from remaining in the regal residence. Instead he preferred the slow wait and see approach, the proven native prognostic methods. He led them to a large window seat, then placed the stack of colorfully illustrated cards on the table.

"Last night I stayed up late playing poker with tarot cards. I got a full house and four people died" (Steven Wright) quipped Dr Gum trying to inject some humor on the subject. Roxy sensed the séance would be anything but comical.

The learned medicine man flipped the first card at random. The FOOL...the figure half man, half animal...running....toward a cliff?

"The fool, heading for a fall. He paused and caught his breath. What he was about to tell them unnerved him inspite of seemingly going through the same spiel each season.

"4 ghosts inhabit this hotel. He was reluctant to suggest anything else much more sinister. A chambermaid, Sara, leapt to her death from the 4th floor into the lobby." Roxy peered out through the stained glass windowed doors into the lobby…. recreating the event in her mind, overcome by a burst of clairvoyance?…her overactive imagination racing.

"Mary, the gal from the gift shop, met a similar fate; she fell from the 6th floor; some say driven to suicide smitten by the hotel manager." They look at him skeptically. "Honest injun."

RD delivered the next detrimental card, CHAOS, a black stallion on it's hind haunches as if rising out of a flaming inferno like a phoenix. "Chaos…" He slowly examined the card. "Could spell trouble, the Killroy burnt to the ground about a year ago. Some of the folks around here still suspect spontaneous combustion." The couple looked at each other…determined to stay for the duration …as long as it took….As he placed the next card…he paused…. "Oh how rude of me, would anyone care for a drink?"

"Thought you'd never ask. Looks like you're well stocked to ride out a long rough winter" said Dr Gum amused by the array of alluring alcoholic bottles. Roxy was preoccupied with the reflection she saw in the window, staring blankly outside, fearing another drinking binge was inevitable.

RD, the hospitable host…eyed the endless array.

"What'll it be?" …He pulled out a particularly old bottle, blew off the dust…the label revealed a 25 year old 80 proof Chivas, a Scotch whiskey dating back 1801, to the mansion in Scotland, the House of Shivas.

"I've been saving this one for my next séance." He poured a couple stiff ones straight. "Live with Chivalry" he announced, the Black Eyed Peas 2009 global campaign. Returning to the table…the two men downed their drinks. Roxy was not amused determined to discover the cause of her odd over whelming feelings…she couldn't quite place a finger on it yet.

"What does this card depict?"

RD took another stiff swig. He looked at the card. 8 OF VESSELS, a miserable wretched beggar fallen to the ground.

"Uh..the drunk, dejected, downtrodden …down on his luck."

"That'll be you, if you keep it up" she said sternly to her husband.

"Honey please, taste it." RD's poured a softer sweeter savory mix for her to sample. She hesitantly lifted the fine Schwarovsky crystal tumbler to her lips.

"Mmmm, a hint of apricots and peaches…"

"A toast to penning a best seller. The place is bound to bring out the beast…uh best in you." The next card revealed was the TEN OF AIR, a menacing vision, ten vultures are gathered around a helpless victim, feasting on his ravaged remains.

"Gathered for the feast."

Dr Gum's insides let out a low dull groan….

"I am rather famished, anyone care to join me… raiding the refrigerator?" The two remained seated as he stepped through the stained glass doorway into the lobby. The persistent rattling of the trapdoor at the top of the space was beginning to bother him. He looked up….and saw that it was open? Like a hangman's trapdoor preparing for it's next victim? He became unhinged.. then hurriedly headed to the kitchen. The large vessel of water was bubbling, boiling over, splashing leaving a slippery tiled floor, and a potentially highly hazardous sheen. He searched the counter and shelves for a coffee maker, but couldn't find one. He felt the upper shelves and located some slippery shiny bags, either chips or...discovered they were a delicious blend of Columbian coffees ....In lieu of the coffee maker, he resourcefully made a 'cheese cloth' type filter from a clean white napkin. He hung the edges of the sheet and placed the empty pot on top of the corners. He quickly emptied the contents of several bags....estimating it's strength, then with several heat resistant oven mitts grabbed the large vessel...as if attempting to pass the 'grasshopper' ritual following a lengthy kung fu training session. The vessel seemed feathery light...as if someone or something was assisting him...he stopped pouring, set it down...and looked around...definitely unnerved.

"Aw, it's nothing." He looked about at his large novel new surroundings, even a quick glance over his shoulder for good measure, then chuckled; just the first night jitters he rationalized to himself.

He left, letting the make shift percolator perform it's mundane task.

In the Weeping Willow lounge RD was about to unveil the next card, the DEATH card, an awful anonymous animal skull, usually a buffalo, accompanied by an owl, a sign of clairvoyance.

"Can I get you some ice?" offered RD, as if sensing a scalding wound to heal? How could he know that? wondered Dr Gum.

"Let me." Roxy felt a little more at ease... as she hopped behind the bar. She marveled at the fresh lemons, fruit, ample supplies, intuitively knowing where her husband would linger for the next couple months. Roxy reached into the stainless steel basin and grabbed an ice pick....then looked around for a chunk. Peering out across the bar, she saw something, in the large floor to ceiling windows. Her reflection? She wasn't sure; and didn't want to alarm anyone, or raise suspicions. She dispelled it to first night butterflies in her new humble abode as she dropped a large chunk....in a bucket....then stirred from her trance. "You were saying?"...no one had said anything...as she approached the table....and dropped a few pieces into their drinks…

"Uh nothing…" noted RD.

"An owl? Yep, that's my husband alright…
a real night owl."

"It's associated with clairvoyance…. next to"
He paused..took a deep breath… "DEATH." RD
rearranged the five cards, placing his hands over
them as one would over a ouija board, then aligned
them into a five pointed star or 'pentacle'. He
began to spook his guests then uttered a remark
…nonsensical? telepathic? communication with the
dead?

"Energy flows where the attention goes"…

Roxy paid close attention, inspite of the slight of
hand …

"That accounts for only three ghosts, doesn't it?
What happened to the 4th?" The two men turned to
her, she wasn't as spaced out or ditsy as was his
first impression of her. One truly mustn't judge a
book by it's cover.

"Indeed."

RD was noticeably uncomfortable as he peered
Around, as if looking right through them…into the
lobby. We see the vision from his perspective. It

takes us into the Stallworthy dining room…then into the kitchen….as if passing through a series of secret doors, deeper into a vault…the recesses of his mind….or either of his captivated audience?

"The chef disappeared…one day…" Never to return. "His wife is still seen wandering around the dining room." He took a stiff swig…to ease his nerves. Roxy detected a bead of perspiration forming on his brow…as if breaking out into a sweat at a native sweat lodge; undecided about what to offer the spirit world to appease the apparitions in his aura. He was in a daze, glassy eyed…Roxy sensed something sinister..

"Rumor has it…. he….chopped her up… dismembered her he did!…never found the body." Dr Gum turned to his dearly beloved….Not the sort of bedtime story he had in mind. He would have preferred something more soothing, sensual, romantic to kindle the flames of desire and set the mood for the evening. Neither was he fully aware of the evil events that had transpired in the retreat. It could explain the eerie sensation and experience; how he could have conceivably 'raised the dead' weight, the heavy bubbling cauldron, on his own.

Roxy was noticeably agitated, thoroughly terrified. Not the opening ceremonies she anticipated.. seriously contemplating packing her bags…but she was much too tired to leave. They'd just have to spend the night now...See how it goes…or she may go.

"I'm ready to retire…I'm bushed." She preferred to leave, politely…without much further a do and delving deeper into the deadly past of the premises. It certainly set a somber, sinister tone…

Dr Gum fished for the remote behind the bar, hoping to catch the late news or Leno…for a few laughs…to alleviate the lingering evil endeavors simmering in the recesses of his subconscious. No reception, left him wondering just how isolated they really were.

"I'll get those" as RD grabbed the glasses in one swift swoop. Likely equally adept at the table cloth trick thought Roxy quietly to herself…Perhaps it was all part of an act? To hype up the 'haunted hotel' mystique?

"No, here let me." She placed her hands on his…and felt a sensation, a surge of something sinister, foreboding…the feeling lingered as she hurried to discard the tumblers in the sink. In lieu of lucky dice, the cards certainly a cause for concern… Had they already sealed their fate? A cool breeze seemed to frisk her legs and extremities; it left her with an uneasy queasy feeling in the pit of her stomach.

"Let me show you to your room. It's a large Lakeview Suite….. on the third floor" urged RD, strained by the day's taxing events. He led them through the drafty lobby to the small metal cage, a cause for alarm for any aspiring claustrophobic. A few lights were left on, scattered about, rather romantic inspite of the rumors, sparing the deadly details. Roxy knew all would be revealed in time. The séance had definitely taken it's toll on RD as he entered the confining enclosure. He could feel it in his bones; much more so than from previous falls. He was woozy on his feet…occasionally brushing into the elegant woodwork or a painting depicting bloodhounds and other festive regal sporting events exclusive to the idle rich.

"Bats in the belfry?" asked the disoriented dentist as RD led them deeper down the dimly lit hallway. He glanced up into the lofty lobby just below the pinnacle, the bell tower, accessible by a narrow set of rather steep stairs…He caught a glimpse of the haunted room up on the 5th floor …Room 512.

"No one's been up to the bell tower for ages. It's all boarded up" then turned and hurried them to their 'honeymoon suite'.

He inserted the key slowly…the lock clicked. He reached inside; fished for the switch. The room erupted in a flash of light as he slowly revealed their regal, sparsely appointed accommodations for the duration of their indeterminate length of their stay. He rushed through into the ensuite, flicked a switch illuminating the master bath. Roxy relished in the regal Victorian furnishings. It was every thing she imagined it would be from the brochure. Dr Gum knew he'd spend but a pittance, a scant proportion of his time here.. as he scanned the stark..solid wood old world charm…Roxy rushed into the master ensuite.

"Even a large old European tub". She unfurled the wrap around shower curtain… and peered into the deep basin void of any visions. She sighed breathing a little easier. Dr Gum was fiddling with a TV, a special request, the extra was set on a large dresser dating back to the early pioneers of the old west.

"NO reception either."

Roxy wound her hand provocatively around the bathroom doorway…

"I'll take your mind off TV."

RD excused himself…caught between a rock and a hard place….

"I'll look into it in the morning."

Roxy emerged excitedly…entranced with the suite.

"Thanks RD, you're a dear."

The humble native host extracted himself from the cozy chamber, then hung a DO NOTDISTURB sign on the ornate door knob then hurried down the dim hallway. He glanced up, over his shoulder periodically, at the historically haunted room, 512… somewhat assured they were in 321. He hurried into the tiny metal cage, as if to provide a false sense of security…from a shark attack for example.…He smiled, then scurried out the front door. It slammed…startling the two lone occupants as he scurried to a separate staff quarters a stone's throw from the main hotel, near the front furrows of freshly turned soil. He was glad to get out of there…and swore to himself not to spend another night in the eerie establishment.

In their room, the wretched relentless reverberation of the trap door unhinged them both…. RD'd have to fix it in the morning!

The final countdown, getting ready for liftoff …rising to the occasion, anticipating no failure to launch, Roxy prepared for the occasion with a provocative skimpy Victoria's secret teddy. She sat at the three sectional vanity mirror applying her secret scents and potions to provoke the savage beast with a contagious concoction of Coco Chanel. The mist mesmerized him as she manicured her fingernails and combed her disheveled hair..like a caged animal, her pent up emotions about to be unleashed….she turned around in the light for a private audition. The light accented her curvaceous features…the sheer wispy outerwear…like a coat of fur about to be shed….

"You can sketch a few provocative charcoal silhouettes of me….if you like…for the book." His mind raced wildly…his fertile imagination found an infinite number of ways to express itself.

"Limitations live only in our minds. But if we use our imaginations, our possibilities become limitless." (Jamie Paolinetti.) he recalled. He'd found the perfect subject matter for his detailed sketch of the assumed…

"An alluring apparition?" She took his breath away. "Come here…where I can see, feel, and hold you." She walked his way seductively.

"Ghosts? Some POW ..WOW!" as she twirled around…in a panoramic eye popping pirouette. They probed each other's presence, unaware of their immediate surroundings anymore, enamored by the intensity of their emotions, focusing all their energy toward one another… preparing for the impending foreplay and lengthy lovemaking. …..'Energy goes where the attention goes' raced through Roxy's mind….Suddenly, they were rudely interrupted, in the midst of their passionate playful antics.. as the radio blared loudly… yet, there was no reception as he flipped himself off her and fumbled with the dials.. she was all revved up.. reeling, getting irritable waiting….as another series of loud boisterous noises, moans and groans, erupted just outside the suite's door. Roxy threw on a terry cloth robe. She rushed to the door …nearly ripped it from it's hinges…perhaps with a little help from the haunting presence she felt …shuffling off down the hall…yet there was no sign of a single soul…Perhaps it was another one of RD's stunts? To set the stage for their haunted honeymoon? To preserve appearances? Prolong the legend as long as possible? perhaps the spirits did not approve of their sensual sordid shenanigans? Or, the apparitions were aroused by the romantic interlude? Their loud courtly love making in the chilly chamber…it reminded her of a castle along the Rhein, off the Scottish moors or Transylvania. The persistent banging of the trap door unhinged her as she peered up into the dark desolate lobby. Satisfied, at least on the surface she looked back into the eerie emptiness then hurriedly hopped back down the hall into the room and under the covers of the preheated sheets….

"RD'll have to fix that first thing. It's driving me nuts." She noticed he'd fallen sound asleep snoring like a grizzly bear settled into hibernation. She looked at her weary wordsmith. "Not if I have anything to say about it." She dived under the covers for her compelling covert operation.

RD was awoken by loud noises coming from the hotel...

"Back at it, huh? feistier than ever?!" he dashed out the door to determine if the couple were alright? Or worse case scenario succumbed to the sinister presence. It was so out of character, uncharacteristic for the 'creature comforts' to emerge so suddenly and rapidly. Normally the evil entity gnawed, slowly over a prolonged period of time, relentlessly, ruthlessly at their sanity, slowly wearing them down, eroding their enthusiasm, defenses, their very minds ...It drove all the others to radical remedies and perilous plans of action in a futile attempt to thwart the ghastly apparition's gruesome game plan. He rushed to the front door... didn't bother to knock nor want to disturb the honeymooners. He looked up to the top of the lofty lobby. Indeed the hangman's trap door was wide open...as if wide awake...waiting for the perfect moment to surprise the unwary...He beelined for the bar...past the monumental rundle rock hearth.

The massive mound…seemed to spring from the very rock of the structure…as an intimate growth…like a vital organ. The bar however was a vestigial organ… most of the wives could take or leave the tempting luxurious elixir, like a malignant tumor….It simply festered, and grew, seeming to feed off their wanton uninhibited ways…their weak willed spirits succumbing to their cravings, satiated the sinister spirit that lurked in the legendary luxurious lodgings. Whatever evil that lurked in the writer's mind eye or imagination paled by comparison, feared RD, as he crept by the giant hearth and mantelpiece, toward the Weeping Willow; where the liquor bottles began to shake rambunctiously as a saber rattling or the amorous rocking and rolling of the amorous couple above, he envisioned.

"Well religion has been passed down through the years by people telling stories around the campfire. Stories about God, stories about love. Stories about good spirits and evil spirits." (Andrew Greeley) They couldn't imagine, in their wildest dreams what lay in store….what lay in the deep dark catacombs of men's minds, hearts and very souls…

He slowly turned out the lights in the lounge… there appeared to be a lapse in the antics, marking the arrival of the lovebirds. The lunacy would continue, escalate he assumed…a full moon was just around the corner…He stopped…stood perfectly still and stretched out his arms…like an ancient ceremonial totem pole…to detect the slightest stirring..it appeared the shenanigans had abated for the evening; all but the batting of the boards above his head…like the banging of the head board up in the honeymoon suite. He had to put an end to the madness once and for all. Drive the nails through the damn decrepit trapdoor…like sealing a sacred sarcophagus, a ceremoniously adorned coffin of a highly revered tribal chief…

 …He paced back and forth in front of the giant hearth. Pondering the other possibility, to torch the terrible temple, the instigator of some of the most gruesome wretched reenactments of the presumed murder of the chef's wife. Perish the thought. He shook his head in disgust, and came to his senses. Who was he to deliberate and deliver such a deadly dose of macabre medicine? The descendent of a long line of legendary native Blackfoot chiefs; it was his duty to preserve the legends…however ludicrous the native tarot cards were perceived by the general public. Bogus baloney or BS to most, he knew deep in his soul, whatever disguised message emerged from the sacred ritual, the deliverance of the medium eventually always revealed itself. Who was he to play with fire? He was simply the timeless messenger…to deliver a dying custom and way of life..as his forefathers had before him. So many souls had succumbed to the senseless slaughter over the years in the relentless pursuit in order to erect the hotel. A monument and tribute to man's conquest of the elements, the environment, and every obstacle set before him. Whatever he conjured up or believed he could conceive, he achieved! Anything…The railroad paved the way and brought the belief in even bigger fortunes to be made. Breaking the ground for the panhandlers pursuing their shattered dreams in the greedy gold rush… All of it came at a tremendous heavy price! The resultant cost of culling countless herds of buffalo, Uprooting reservations in laying the routes…the annihilation of adversaries including his own fellow flesh and blood Blackfoot…left an anger and eerie emptiness in his heart down to his very soul. He sought to seek the truth.. in the eyes of each of the new arrivals, the windows to their soul….for some answers, some inherent good…and to warn them. He sought long and hard….It was a futile search like the quest for the irrevocable sinister presence that had lodged itself deep inside the walls, the very grounds. It was more than mere ghosts, the curiosity of the occasional occult chaser. It was indelibly planted, perhaps as deep as the…… permafrost? But it had grown stronger over the years….seeking out it's victims. As man once did as he roamed the desolate barren plains and mesa in his blood thirsty quest to quench his appetite… to consume…to conquer…. to search for souls to slaughter, senselessly ….merely because they were in his way! Grover Cleveland's amendment to repeal protected cherished native stomping grounds, appeasing James J. Hill's haughty hopes of erecting the high class hilltop hacienda…were realized alright. Perhaps the hotel, in a most macabre way, was mediating, not by mitigating the messy crimes of the past, but meddling in the very affairs of mice and men that tread on the sacred ground? Treading in territory that did not belong to them or concern them….Perhaps it was the reason why the hotel lay dormant for most of the year, like a haughty hibernating beast? Only to awaken for a few short weeks…to forage and feast fervently on the few meager offerings to cross it's path? Like the simple spiritual offerings in the sweat lodge. RD grabbed his small medicine pouch that hung loosely around his neck and clenched it tightly, to prepare for the worst…it would be one winter he'd likely never forget.

3: Unwrapped

"Vision without execution is
    hallucination."
                - Thomas Edison

The fingers of light danced on the morning dew
sending a radiant sunburst off the frosty shingled
rooftop and window sills. They slowly crept into
the silent Lakeview Suite....and frisked the forlorn
faces of the two occupants; then warmed the silk
threads of the fine covers in a spider web like
geometric pattern. The first night took it's toll, the
endless tossing and turning eventually transitioned

into a few hours of desperately needed deep REM sleep for the couple. A gentle rapping at the door startled Roxy. She jumped from the bed …refreshed, yet equally frightened…would the relentless irritable spirits ever quit? As she peered out the picturesque frosty window pane she realized the nightmare had ended. Morning, the break through she sought…refreshed her…. invigorated her with renewed strength.

The knocking persisted. She hurriedly wrapped a POW embroidered terry cloth robe around her warm body to preserve the soothing heat then tip toed to the door. A priceless Navajo weaving provided additional warmth on her feet. Her hand reached for the door hesitantly.

"Room service." The familiar voice set her at ease. "Morning sleepy heads." Roxy opened the door to greet the gentle jack of all trades turned waiter as well. He entered the suite with a silver platter of delicious aromatic delights…then set it down on the table for two near the window. Roxy opened the exquisite designer drapes...as her husband came around.

"Thought you might like an early start….You

know what they say?"…they waited for his words of wisdom anxiously….he smiled, chuckled; adding "Early bird gets the worm….not many days like this left." They sighed at his rather mundane remark. The temperamental weather conditions in Wutherington were renown for radical changes.

"I can feel it in my bones" said Roxy as she shuddered…pulling the robe's drawstring tightly around her waist. Her hungry husband joined her at the table. Staring into her sleepy bedroom eyes, he slowly lifted the silver cover. Both averted their gaze momentarily…to what awaited them. Fragrant slabs of bacon, some unfamiliar form of freshly caught venison perhaps? sunny side up eggs, a few slices of toast, special preserved POW jams and jellies; and a sprinkling of garnish. Combined with the fresh brewed blend of coffee and cream, gave their taste buds the kick start they needed. They devoured their breakfast. Roxy then rushed into the ensuite….and ran the hot water…she slowly lowered her robe, then wrapped the thin veil around the tub….she's lost in thought, lathering her body, savoring the sweet soapy fragrance and soothing drops of radiant heat. "better keep yourself clean and bright, for you are the window through which you must see the world." (George Bernard Shaw) resonated through her mind as the persistent spray prickled her soft skin. Dr Gum tiptoed toward the dresser fishing through the drawers. He hurriedly grabbed the surprise then slowly approached the shower curtain, her curvaceous provocative silhouette aroused him…

"Honey is that you?" He wondered who else would it be? as he swept the sheer curtain aside and stepped inside….and raised his arm. She breathed a sigh of relief as his arm swiftly sliced down her back…. with a giant soapy sponge…she cooed from the massaging motion tracing her torso…. Renewed, ready for come what may, they quickly dressed in casual jeans and Cashmere sweaters… Took one last sip of coffee then cautiously enter the hallway. A difference of night and day, the sounds of silence instead of the naughty night marish neighbors that unnerved them all night long.

Dr Gum cruised through the vacant void…then planted himself at the elegant ebony desk. As he peered out over the lake, an icy mist rose from it's surface; he noticed the Miss Wutherington was missing. He had hoped to take in a booze cruise.

"Tucked her in for the winter?" as he intuitively recognized RD's heavier moccasin muted footsteps advance.

"The Miss Wutherington…settled down for a long winter's nap." RD brought the laptop, compliments of the POW, with a tangled web of power cord connectors. The antiquated aging hotel was so remote, wireless was unheard of. Why, he recalled a remark by Steven Wright: 'I stayed in a really old hotel last night. They sent me a wake up letter.'…

A blood curdling scream pierced the cathedral like silence coming from the direction of the kitchen. Both men bolted for the source of the obnoxious noise. Roxy stood before a large freezer door….her icy fingers still shook…the cool gust left a rash of goose bumps all over her arms and presumably the peek a boo parts. Blood was dripping from the fresh venison from the upper levels of the voluminous space, large enough to accommodate a couple comfortably. Dr Gum hurried over to hold her icy cold hands ….

…rubbing them relentlessly.

"Don't be alarmed, I took some fresh venison from the freezer…shot it a couple days ago."

Dr Gum examined the large slabs of flesh with his eyes. Definitely a massive beast, must be indigenous he determined.

"Buffalo?"

"Heart best, right after the kill" remarked RD, nodding, leaving little doubt about his skills in marksmanship. The tradition of extracting the heart of the buffalo went back to Blackfoot tradition about the time the first park wardens appeared.

"Thought steak dinner…for the inner….circle." They had their reservations about the odd description of the item on the menu, but would learn to live with RD's unique approach to making them feel welcome. And to appease Roxy's craving to concoct and hone her culinary craft, he excitedly uncovered a collection of cardboard boxes labeled POW, marked Christmas/Hanukah decorations. In anticipation of a long stay and something for her to do to while away the weeks of wanton idleness.

"Thanks RD, I don't know what I'd do without you." Roxy reached out for him and gave him a big bear hug much to the chagrin of her husband. He thought the gesture was far too generous and much too time consuming. She detected a hint of jealously…

"Well, I'll leave you two…I'll be around the hotel….pokin' about." He disappeared without a trace or sound.

Dr Gum greedily helped his wife unwrap the goodies…as if opening house warming gifts from a shower, or a sneak peek at carefully selected Christmas gifts ready to wrap. They rummaged through the extensive collection of culinary implements, cookie cutters, rolling pins, blenders, cutlery, mixing spatulas, even an ornate chocolate fountain…fondue forks and so on.

He found a large fluffy chef's hat…and placed it on his head. His wife was amused by a silly apron that read "Kiss the Bloomin' Onion' with a large sliced sphere strategically placed below the belt. Outback's original entrée…an imaginatively incised onion, filleted like a flower, slowly brought to a boil in oil to bring out all the flavors of the object. At Chili's it was called the Awesome Blossom and ranked as America's worst appetizer. A possible predictor of her cooking skills? She was in better spirits and soon amusing herself dreaming up ways to delight her husband with devilishly decadent desserts. He departed, leaving the large chef's hat next to the deep fryer…to immerse himself in mapping out the subconscious messages and hidden meanings of his manuscript. The two were left to tango and tackle their own distinct challenges in their arena, perhaps not an area of expertise…time would tell.

"To thine own self be true." (Shakespeare)

"Hmmm, I might make a mountain of Christmas cookies." She delved deeper into the disarray of recipe cards, books, and assortment of accessories. Short on bread but not ideas, she sliced into the large bags of sifted flour in a frenzy… sending a white fluffy cloud into the air…Roxy arranged a series of descendingly deeper mixing bowls on the endless stainless steel counter. She spread the pans out..soon the place was looking like a prepping assembly line for some of the former gala festive events. The entertaining suarreys and shin digs of the sophisticated socialites who graced the hotel with their presence in the past. Or in the event of unexpected visitors, she'd have an enticing tray of treats to serve throughout the festive season and well into spring. She'd take care of their needs, fatten them up alright..like the wicked witch that preyed on the unsuspecting Hansel and Gretl?

Dr Gum seated himself behind the large ebony desk, the size of a small runway, or aircraft carrier deck clear for takeoff. The very dense wood sank in water and was found in Egyptian tombs. He looked out and imagined a vast sea of distinguished guests. Gathered, mingling, discussing their sordid stories of the day. The Great Gatsby era of envious evocative events and illicit affairs. The brandy snifters hot, onto the scent of another scandal? The aromatic virgin's thighs rolling the tobacco leaves, left doubt in his fertile imagination; those decadent days were here to stay…forever. He peered at the elegant old player piano in the opposite corner. Composed, waiting to unravel a compelling concerto or raunchy vaudeville tune. His mind was ready to unwrap and depict an epic event. Rummaging through the catacombs of his

voluminous virtual vault, he carefully selected
the necessary ingredients. The mighty pen would
once again dispel the myth and prove it's power
over the cold steel surface of a sword. He began to
tap the keys in a frenzy….letting his thoughts take
him where they will… 'where the energy flows
…the soul only knows.' The keys on the ebony
desk grew warm to the touch by the continuous
tapping…as the ivory in the hands of a gifted
concert pianist, crafting a complete concerto in his
head. His wife preoccupied, compiling a fiesta
resistance, the icing on the cake? Their inspiration
came from God only knew where, but the POW
hotel seemed to be bringing out the best in them.

Outside, RD was wielding a sharp axe. The dried
wood severed quickly as his muscular arms
brought the wrath of the weapon down upon the
logs and massive tree trunk chopping block.. The
sections served the insatiable appetite of the blast
furnace…soon belching smoke at full bore. He
knew winter would be upon them early this year.
He peered out over the lake, then down to the all
but deserted desolate town…there was no sign of
life. He marveled the massive monument, peering

up to the prominent pinnacle, the bell tower, then refocused on a few upper floors. It left him with a chill. A few residents eyed his every move. Dr Gum was getting into his groove.... Ideas beginning to gel... 'the hotel seemed to have a spirit, a mind of it's own...the four ghosts, guardians of the gates', he paused; were they simply guests? granted the privilege of a private performance to something much more sinister.... His thoughts turned to his wife.

"Ouuuuuuch!" The words resonated in the amazing ambience of the cathedral sized acoustic chamber. The persistent distractions began to bother him. Reluctantly he rushed through the Stallworthy dining space..into the kitchen.

"Damn it, what is it this time?"

Roxy had cut herself on the razor sharp edge of an animal shaped cookie cutter. The steel form lay on the floor....amongst a small red rivulet of her blood. Her gaping wound dripped onto the white canvas on the countertop, filling the flour with a multitude of erratic ruby red etchings that trickled off the edge. Each drop emanated on the endless tiled floor clanging, reverberating like a cacophany of rattling pots and pans as it was allowed to amplify and become the center and focus of his attention. Like the persistent trapdoor it could conceivably drive them both nuts! He rushed to wrap her finger in an elegantly embroidered POW napkin he grabbed from an unpacked box nearby. Roxy became fixated on her fingers…frozen, petrified, still shuddering in a state of shock. As he held her tight, an aura , an overwhelming sense of clairsentience came over her. She peered at her phantom digits, her missing fingers. Lopped off, a war wound? the price paid by a prisoner of war? The clarity of the feeling and touching premonition unnerved her, unsure of what was happening to her she didn't recognize him as he shook her…

"Roxy, it's meeeee."

She shuddered…his grip unrelenting. Finally she snapped out of it attributing the episode to some thing she ate? Food poisoning? She felt her fore head, she wasn't running a fever.

"Clumsy me…I'll be fine."

Her culinary skills left a lot to be desired. He didn't expect this, nor need this distraction. Not now. He despised the thought of taking her into town, or possibly all the way to the ER in Buffalo Butte…but obviously 'the best laid plans of mice an men gang aft agley.' (Robert Burns) She encouraged him not to worry and entertain his demons…deliver the drama, have a drink and plough ahead. Relieved at her diametrically opposed demeanor, he disappeared in the direction of his desk. Nothing seemed to dissuade them from their tasks at hand.

He pounded the laptop tabs relentlessly as much as she needed to purge her pent up energy to the point of ecstatic exhaustion from a surge in endorphin release following her foolish mishap. She kneaded and massaged the mountain of dough to the point of desperation…as if driving the living daylights out of some surreal or…. imagined ingredient. Delicately, yet deliberately she began to imagine then made the mini parts of a mansion. Her meticulous attention to detail, as she mapped out the miniscule window sashes, walls, balconies, railings, was amazing. An array of doughy gooey pre fab parts like a giant jigsaw puzzle took up most of the counter space. She had disassembled a magnificent architectural monstrosity in her mind's eye. Now the challenging task of piecing together the 3D puzzle. The exquisite exploded diagram that she envisioned was slowly taking shape.

"A gingerbread house?" marveled the king of the castle. His clever, talented companion stopped to analyze her add ons. Her latent talents, the likes of which tickled his fancy left him floored as she tried to figure out the rest of the floor plan. He definitely distracted her now.

"I can't do anything right" as she eyed her unfinished fiasco. He looked at her hand, commenting,

"Just be more careful next time." He was alarmed by all the ovens on at once…the deep fryer spitting out boiling oil…the temperature rising, the risk of a fire first and foremost on his mind. Could she be trusted with the cutlery? The massive stoves? Would she burn down the house?

"If you can't stand the heat, get outta the kitchen." Her tone and expression were suddenly much meaner. It was so out of character for her to snarl at him…yet she remained on the defensive peering at the sharp cleavers just in case. Then snapped out if it…suddenly. "Sorry sweetie." Her bizarre behavior bewildered him as he backed out of the kitchen hesitantly. He had to trust her, give her a chance to redeem herself…as he set about his business, going full bore.

The time flew….she put her chef's hat back on… hurrying to erect the regal hacienda…and clean up the unimaginable mess in her culinary laboratory. She turned the ghetto blaster on loud, blaring like a bloody live rock concert, or barking out like a declaration or royal decree for all the town folk to hear….. 'Moonlight on the water

> sunlight on my face
>
> you and me together
>
> we are in our place
>
> The gods are in the heavens
>
> Angels treat us well
>
> Oracle has spoken
>
> We cast the perfect spell'

He can't hear himself think…getting snarly disturbed by the shock waves pounding on his ear drums.

> 'The King is in the countin room
>
> countin all the money

The Queen is in the kitchen

Makin bread and honey

No friends and yet no enemies

Absolutely free….

No rats aboard the magic ship

Perfect harmony…'

(John Lennon – 'Clean Up Time' lyrics)

Roxy was manically manipulating the pieces of the 3D puzzle in the countless bread pans; the monstrous mansion would soon take shape, all the pieces falling into place. While he tapped like a mad man, his limber digits dancing over the keyboard like a woodpecker wired from wood alcohol? He was in a daze, didn't bother to read or review his words. He'd go over it later. Where had the afternoon gone?

Roxy prepared a decadent dessert while the structure set. Her curiosity could not be contained as she unpacked the chocolate fountain. She chipped large chunks of chocolate with an ice pick like a crazed sculpture…then immersed them in a boiling cauldron in lieu of a hot cup of cocoa or tea. The chocolate lake of lava began to bubble as another idea popped into her head. She sliced and diced an assortment of fruits and vegetables for a colorful, flavorful fondue. She found the pot at the end of the long counter…keeping one eye on the hand crafted mini mansion parts through the portholes into the intense inferno. She figured a frosty coating, a fitting finishing touch to compliment her efforts; for the grand finale! Her husband was aroused by the aroma that permeated the palace and lingered in the lobby, then left to investigate her inventions.

"The bread man cometh" he commented confident he'd pen a monumental best seller.

Roxy removed some of her clothing in the sweltering sauna like conditions, covered and caked in chocolate. It was difficult to determine where the cook ended and the cooking began. She was the canvas, a sensual work in progress…

"My…my sugar mama!" he chuckled, tempted to lick the chocolate from every square inch of her statuesque torso. He approached her like a rabid dog…Pavlov's pet? his wet tongue salivating, wagging eager to lick her face.

"Down boy!" she barked, pushing him away, then wheeled the tea cart like a trained stewardess along the aisle and into the lounge. She rolled it toward the window and offered her little devil a small fork. The bubbling cauldron of chocolate, the centerpiece, sat in the middle of bite sized morsels of fruit and crouton bread cubes.

"Let's take it nice and slow" as she passed the fork to him. The proper etiquette was not to double dip the bread into the bubbling cauldron. To touch the fork was a faux pas. The penalty, promptly buy a bottle of wine from the bar.

"I'll get the bottle" he said, familiar with the custom after he dropped his bread into the chocolate bath following the fast pitch. Later, several bottles strewn around the table; they were both caked in chocolate. Roxy disappeared behind the bar...to select a special tune....a dark chocolate extremity provocatively appears from behind the bar.

"Baby take off your coat....

real slow....

baby take off your shoes...

I'U take off your shoes....

She slipped out of her Sperry topsiders, the chocolate slowly flaking off...

baby take off your dress…

yes, yes, yes….

She slipped out of her chocolate covered dress and apron, the dark 'tan' on her extremities still evident.

You can leave your hat on….

You can leave your hat on….

You can leave your hat on…..

Still wearing her chef's hat….

Go over there, turn on the lights..

All the lights….

She turned down the dimmer switch.

Come back here, stand on that chair..

She complied…on the frigid chocolate fringe..
Wobbly but wouldn't fall down….

Get up there, that's right

Raise your arms in the air..

And now shake'em..

Chocolate lava rained down on him like a bleeding volcano, after all on everyone a little rain must fall!
She was now shivering in her birthday suit!

You give me reason to live

You give me reason to live….

You give me reason to live….

You give me reason to live….

(Joe Cocker, 'You Can Keep Your Hat on' lyrics)

He reached up and took her hand, ushering her into his arms to lick the lingering lava coating of chocolate leftovers from every sq. inch of her lovely skin….as they lay by the window peering out into the vast desolate emptiness…a menacing icy cold front crept in from the far end of the lake as they dropped out of sight. Mt Cloverfield, the tallest peak in the park, was completely obscured, shrouded in a veil of frost. Their vision blurred, from lengthy lovemaking, the windows were all steamy, making it impossible to discern the imminent advancing snowstorm. He hustled her through the lobby wearing only a table cloth …hesitantly she checked to see if the coast was clear…then cautiously dashed for the cage. The two love birds, prisoners of their unbridled passion, packed into the protective enclosure. His cute little canary chirped, and persisted to peck his cheek in the cage eager to get to the sanctuary for another round of decadent desserts…they let their animal instincts take over as they raced down the hall to the presumptuous safety of their room.

Roxy tossed the table cloth aside and rushed into the ensuite. She drew a large bubble bath …then slipped into the dark bubbling liquid, a special select shade of ass's milk, her torso tingled, as the effervescent tiny chocolate bubbles rose all around her…her pores became permeated with the pure rich dark blend of emollients and exclusive nutrients. She remained immersed in her private baptismal font, savoring the soothing life renewing salts, like the pool at Bethesda for an eternity. … a flavorful human fondue….Roxy waited for the right moment to taunt and tease her husband relentlessly with another bite of the irresistible treat. Slowly, she stepped out of the soothing bath. Her favorite, a dark chocolate flavored film, enveloped her body in a warm radiant coat like airy light feathers…for once in her life she felt free, unfettered by all their imposed man made restrictions that bound her. The chains of her mortal existence and preconceived inhibitions were broken by the unbelievable experience, and idyllic getaway. If only everyone could've shared in the fun and free for all. The sheer freedom, and loftiness of being…she twirled around again and

again in a state of near nirvana and ecstasy
hoping the moment would never end…

But as all good things must come to an end
…that's why it's called an end…she eased herself
unrelentingly onto her husband one more time….
….for the time of their lives…like his favorite aero
filled chocolate bar, all unwrapped, he savored the
sweet taste that always left him craving for more.
The proverbial deceptive Barbie doll like hard shell
exterior gave way to a soft, sensitive intoxicating
interior. Beauty was only skin deep. After all,
'words are only postage stamps delivering the
object for you to unwrap' (George Bernard Shaw)
She was a priceless volume that held it's secrets
concealed, the cover but a mere miniscule nano
fraction of what was truly lurking inside. For a
brief moment, they were lost in the lap of luxury,
like time travelers unaware of their place or
position…perhaps in a parallel suspended state of
animation….

RD certainly felt their presence, amongst the
privileged people…like some unsavory spoiled
rock stars….trashing their accommodations
following a frenzied performance on stage,

fulfilling their fan's fantasies. They'd certainly fulfilled theirs as he scanned the disaster zone in the Weeping Willow lounge… as if a bomb had burst in a Bernard Callebaut boutique chocolate shop or a large shaggy St Bernard had shaken himself off on the furniture, following a romp and a roll in the muddy grounds outside. He fought back the tears as he planned the best course of action to eradicate the evidence of their decadent interlude. RD intended to leave the premises spotless; he didn't need an 'incident' to tarnish his …perfect track record, not now! ..albeit, all but a few unexplained bodies over the years that turned up unannounced. He feared the POW management may have his hide, leave it out to tan. They had to come clean with him…to treat their castle as their as they would their own home. With a little more respect, genuine TLC and for God sakes, care for their surroundings and remove their litter as any one camping out in the regal residence were expected to do so. The ramifications would reverberate and could be felt through out the park. If everyone left a lingering trail of litter, and seek to spread their unsightly refuse, the park authorities

would refuse to allow anyone to enter. Perhaps
it was for the better? A place as palatial as this
required an army of maintenance workers and
gardeners to tend to it's up keep. Like a Hollywood
mansion, the monstrous bills mounted each
season, come rain or shine just to keep the POW
open. Perhaps it were best returned to nature? Let
the POW slowly slip back into it's natural state
…let the mansion acquire all the moss of a rolling
stone? In time the crumbling, moth eaten structure
would implode on itself, erode away with the
seasons …the harsh contrast would ultimately take
it's toll and reduce the dilapidated, decrepit,
decomposing structure to rubble…and rudimentary
debris…from ashes to ashes, dust to dust…a
conservation of kinetic energy he postulated. He
ruminated the rather novel idea as he removed the
tell tale signs of his guests. They were a disgrace,
becoming more of a burden than the four ghosts.
At least they left no tell tale signs other than their
regular mundane routine of bells and whistles.
One could practically set one's watch by the
rigorous routine.. like a long winded outdated
vaudeville act…he hoped their batteries would

soon run down like everybody else. And their boisterous, at times obnoxious presence, kept at bay. He continued to scour the chairs and carpet for the trail of carnage…occasionally peering out on Enchanted Bay…it appeared as if a thin slick sheen had formed on the surface. He knew now, that a long cold winter was imminent indeed. RD prepared to batten down the hatches and sharpen the hatchet to fill the hearth with firewood. With each passing year he placed less confidence on the old boiler. He decided to take a stroll down stairs.

4: Seasons

"Even bees, the little almsmen of spring
bowers know there is richest juice in
poison flowers."
- John Keats, English romantic poet

The composed couple, deceptively dapper from
their dynamic deserved interlude descended down
the stairs….taking their time to tidy up, she fixed
his small bow tie, then primped her black evening
gown. Preoccupied with appearances they seemed
to saunter down the grand staircase as if to deliver
a presidential address, or make a fashionably late
entry to an evening of fun filled festivities or New

Years ball. They paused as they entered the large desolate lobby and looked around. Dr Gum detected a distinct aroma once again. It was not the tempting tobacco leaves but rather the odor of burning baked goods! Roxy shuffled through the Stallworthy dining room as best she could without tearing the fine few threads which tenuously supported her gown. Her quick small strides reminded him of a geisha girl, perhaps in anticipation of another encore song and dance performance, her face caked in a fine film of white flour as before? He watched her moving and shaking her fresh buns through the narrow side entry way. She hurriedly scanned the counter…and found a few 'buffalo' shaped cookies. The symbol of provider, great healing power, also polygamy…. A male of the species is renown for removing any rivals, running them down and chasing them away. As she reached over to pop another tray of short bread cookies into the massive oven, she noticed a seam of smoke seeping from the perimeter of the door. The burnt offerings, the source of the smell.. She peered into the window struck by the odd sticky gooey substance that flowed from the

surface of the sections of the gingerbread house.
She couldn't recall layering any of the pieces with
chocolate. As she slowly opened the door in
increments of inches to let the fans fumigate the
prep area, she glanced at the glazing. A sense of
utter shock overcame her, another clairvoyance
episode, then slammed the door. Her baking was
not covered in chocolate at all, but seemed to ooze
a thick bloody red substance. Indeed it was blood
dripping from the sections of the baked building.
She grabbed a rag, and maniacally wiped the
surface of the counter….she feared she was losing
her mind, but made no qualm to alarm her
husband. He'd likely commit her if she revealed
her shocking revelation. She'd let him have a look,
see it with his own eyes and allow him to
corroborate and confirm her suspicion. She turned
up the volume on the ghetto blaster to help ease her
edginess, her gyrations grew, then grew some
more…prompted by her gruesome discovery.

> 'Now it begins, let it begin….
> Clean up time…hey, hey….
> Clean up time, well, well, well…
> However far we travel

Where ever we may roam

The center of the circle

Will always be our home

Yeah, yeah, yeah….

Clean up time

Clean up time

Clean up time

Clean up time.'

(John Lennon, 'Clean Up Time' lyrics)

RD ran into the kitchen then stopped dead in his tracks, startled by the volume, and her wild violent scrubbing action…as she moved along the counter. Dr Gum rushed to hold her….to help her get a hold of herself…something had certainly stirred her deeply. Inspite of the expenditure of energy following their passion play he was surprised to see her so charged, energized. She'd obviously been running around the hotel, perhaps jogging along the marked trails to town but….as he touched her she was overwhelmed by the same sinister frightening feeling, a case of clairsentience once again?

"I can't feel a thing" she blurted out.

"After that earth shattering orgasm…I don't

blame you" he boasted.

"Can't you be serious?" she said ornerily, the sudden split personality shocked him…RD stood silently nearby. Her imagination was running away with her again or … were her legs and arms disappearing? She looked blankly at them, both her limbs were gone, phantom limbs…as if she were turning into a ghost….from a previous injury?

"Now is the winter of our discontent' thought her husband. He held her arms tightly. Her whole body was trembling. Heaven forbid she'd toy with the idea of splitting up?

"Where's my arm?" she screamed.

"Are you pulling my leg?" he responded. She grabbed a knife but didn't see her hand It appeared to float in mid air….was she going mad? She was making wild thrusts….sweeping motions with a very sharp implement.

"Get away from me! You hear me?"

He held her from behind…just out of reach of the razor sharp edge flailing about..

Her voice became a sinister deep tone. She was snapping, sensed the two stunned spectators.

"What's gotten into you?"

"You…." she paused and took a deep breath. "won't anymore!"

"Roxy, be reasonable, look at yourself!" She was a mess… "Listen to yourself." Shaking, she bent over and peered into the oven once again. He slowly released her….as she seemed to settle down, slowly opening the metal door like a drawbridge, the fire breathing dragon….belching out a nauseous toxic cloud of smoke. All she could see were rivers of blood oozing from the carefully crafted gingerbread components….she looked at him with a macabre blank stare…she cracked a crazy wide smile then tried to expel a gust, some thing from within, straight from her gut as if to say seeeeeeee? …but remained speechless.

Both of the eyewitnesses wondered what the commotion was about as the smoke dissipated. The cookies were miraculously unmarred, not the cinder blocks or charred remains they both imagined from the wretched smell. Perhaps a gas leak surmised RD. he'd look into it right away. Roxy remained in a state of surreal suspended animation…she wondered if she were fading away..a fateful sign or omen? What was this strange sign? The recurring image of missing limbs, a message? Perhaps she was becoming a time traveler? Permitted only a short passage in this place and dimension. Destined to disappear; their short but sweet honeymoon over with no hope of a future together. She needed time and her space to mull a million things over. Dr Gum was concerned, chilled to the core, not even venturing a guess as to what came over her. It did however fuel his fertile vivid imagination as he let her be and bolted to the corner of the lobby. The laptop lured him, seemed to beckon him, to unveil his deepest darkest insights. To purge his persistent pressing urges, to elaborate on everything he had just witnessed. He began to pound the keys in a furious frenzy….filling up page after page with his word perfect vocabulary….Dr Gum was in a trance, yet looked at the two together…through the doorway. What was RD doing just standing there? why couldn't he fix something? albeit his wife was the one who seemed to need a major overhaul! A wave of rage and jealousy surged through his body. It was so unlike him. He had to purge these feelings by continuing to pound on the keyboard…nearly breaking the tabs. He was delighted by his word smithing… like a belligerent blacksmith, he attacked it. 'All's fair in love and war' he fumed. He typed like a madman, a 'bat out of hell'…. Occasionally stopping to consider the syntax…a missing vowel…the arrangement of consonants in the cleverly crafted expose. He felt confident everything was falling into place. Pleased with his performance and prolific output, a burst from where he did not know, nor venture a guess, he paused. The persistent rattling of the trapdoor unhinged him.

"Damn it RD, can't you do anything right?" he blurted out audibly…although RD was out of ear shot, still seemingly surprised by the split personality of his wife. He figured he'd do it himself. Can't wait for spring. The trapdoor was driving him nuts! RD ran through the lobby, still fuming, shaking his head. He couldn't believe the couple was transforming so fast right before his eyes. They'd only been in the hotel for a couple days. What would they be like in a couple weeks? months? Certainly wasn't cabin fever, there was plenty of room to roam. Why a buffalo could….

He stopped dead in his tracks…then turned around. Dr Gum was nowhere to be found. Odd…the permanent fixture was missing. His curiosity piqued he silently snuck up on the laptop, anxious to take a peek at the progress of the author.

RD was stunned…..as he backspaced, fast forwarded the pages….the entire passage was nothing more than the ominous message….

K I L L R O _ Y….

over and over and over and over again…..
he couldn't believe what he saw!

RD peered up into the rafters of the rickety old regal residence…and declared defiantly.

"Not these two!" He was startled, noticing the trap door ajar, no open. A face appeared from within….

Dr Gum poked his proboscis through the small aperture. He nearly lost his balance…dizzy from the height but grabbed the perimeter planking …carefully balancing with both arms along the two adjacent edges. It was still large enough to swallow anyone whole and send them to their death in a dramatic crushing fatal 7 story fall or torn to bits, sliced and diced like grated cheese by several tiers of flesh tearing razor sharp circles of the giant wagon wheel like chandelier. He overcame his dizziness rapidly as a wave of adrenaline shot through his body. His gaze fixated on the dark figure hunched over the large black desk like an aircraft on final approach, taxing toward the tarmac. 'X marks the spot' he said sternly to himself…perturbed by the prying eyes of Pocahontas…or rather chief Powhatan, her father, the big cheese himself; a powerful confederacy of tribes in Virginia. Relations between the natives and the colonists soured shortly after his death in 1618 as his brother, Opechancanough, sought to drive away the English. Black slaves oft joined the tribes in rebellion against their former captors…. Many became servants through the 18th century. Perhaps it was an ironic twist of fate that he served in the palatial premises? The title of Pocahontas, meaning frolicsome wanton nature, may best be bestowed upon Roxy he reasoned. The vivacious temperamental rabble rouser…was reason enough to carefully extract himself from his precarious predicament and not end up at the wrong end of the hangman's noose! He noticed RD did nothing to remedy the racket as he slammed the rickety old wood. He'd have RD's hide…. Then he noticed a narrow passageway..leading to nowhere..or..to find out he carefully unscrewed a light bulb and inched down the dark hall.. then screwed it in to get a better look at the secret passage in the artificial light….several steep steps led into an upper chamber…via an even narrower slit…also marked by empty light receptacles…he carefully removed the hot bulb…tossing it like a hot potatoe….then quickly inserted it into the socket at the pivotal juncture. Curious, he climbed the near vertical steps causing an acute case of claustrophobia. He wasn't surprised by the fact the trap door over his head opened with little effort. The bright natural light brought a whole new perspective to the narrow niche…dusty stale cobwebs lined the route…making the transition deceptively dangerous. He thrust the escape hatch open then climbed out…like a medieval parapet or watch tower he was granted a spectacular 360 degree panoramic snap shot. A great idea for the book he thought to himself. All 4 seasons seemed to blend into one as he perused the lay of the land. The white capped peaks, the rich green carpet…with a light frosting at the upper levels, the greener hues down below…the ripe orange and blood red hues of harvest…and the subtle yellow spots hinting at spring. "Every season has it's peaks and valleys. What you have to try to do is eliminate the Grand Canyon." (Andy Van Slyke) he rationalized. Roxy was simply spooked by her new surroundings, going a little stir crazy …but nothing to be alarmed about as he took a deep breath. The sound of footsteps below him unnerved him…No one knew about the bell tower except RD…About to call her name, he climbed down to greet his ghostly guest …when RD appeared out of the dark…

"Could get yourself killed up here..if you don't watch your step!" with heavy emphasis on kill… overkill in fact.

"Yeah, it's an open and shut case" remarked the dentist sternly as he pointed to the trapdoor.

"What the…? I nailed that shut."
Dr Gum looked at him skeptically…if looks could kill.

"I'd keep a little distance from the misses…" as he looks down into the lobby. "She's a bleedin' volcano…about to go off.".he paused

"Something's set her off. It's the hotel isn't it?"
A blood curdling howl shattered the serene
silence….

"They're hungry" says RD in a sinister tone….
The dentist is not sure how to take that comment..
The wolves waiting for anyone to take a walk away
from…or something lurking within the hotel?

"Oh, by the way doc….at a loss for words? Or
just the booze talkin'?..I'd take a walk…. down to
the lake…clear your head…..it works for me."
And get him out of the way, place him in harm's
way with the wolves wondered the perceptive
practitioner…practiced in the art of persuasion..

"I'll keep that in mind. Just mind your own
affairs." He was still perturbed by the pesky
Powhaten pokin' around his paperwork. RD was
definitely approachin' his property, as far as he
was concerned, only Roxy was permitted to keep
her hat on at the POW. The aspiring writer was the
chief of his own affairs; only she'd rest her head
on his shoulders. They went their separate ways at
the bottom of the stairs. RD turned to tend to more
important matters, maintain the main boiler and

desperately keep up to the demand. The ominous cold front, a harbinger of frighteningly frigid weather…the stormbringer'd likely leave a load of snow on their doorstep.

"Bound to be a big dump tonight…maybe a foot or two."

"Blackfoot prognosis?"

"The longer we linger here, the more likely we are to tear each other's eyes out."

"We'll see" said RD omnipotently.

Dr Gum returned to his laptop. He was floored as he flipped through several pages of his work. He wondered what he was thinking at the time but drew a blank. He looked about, then turned toward the Weeping Willow lounge. He entered it at his own risk. He needed a stiff drink to relax, take his mind off the macabre messages….wondering what was happening to him.

"The POW getting to me?…or am I the POW? …that must've been… "some POW WOW!" as he relived the provocative performance by his private dancer over again in his mind. Certainly not grounds to get upset or get rid of her…was it?

Roxy raised the bar, intending to complete her

puzzling 3D dilemma as she removed the bloody red stained assortment of baked ginger bread parts from the blast furnace. Like sticky steel slabs..the blood seemed to act as a fixative..as she stacked them higher and higher....like a crane at a high rise construction site in some sort of order of assembly. Then methodically, she began to erect the monumental engineering marvel, room by room, floor by floor. There seemed to be a genuine genius or borderline madness to her method as she brought the project to fruition. Oddly enough, rather than some random relic or historic house or fairytale castle, it resembled a hotel. Not just any hotel, THE hotel...the POW! It was an unbelievable work in progress, but there was no doubt, she'd made a miniature macabre model down to the last detailed doorway and window sash. The only discernible difference that became bloody obvious to anyone blind as a bat was the eerie elevated, bas relief of the blood that continued to seep and ooze from every orifice of the replica. The rather chilling culinary craftsmanship shocked her...as she stared at the blood soaked sections...she found no evidence of blood on her fingertips…because she couldn't find them! The sections seemed to float into place all by themselves…by telepathic power? Mind over matter? She didn't mind; she'd already lost it she assumed...as she stared off into space.…she had to get a grip…get a hold of herself. What'll happen to me, a week hence? The weekend getaway for two was turning into a nightmare. Nothing made sense anymore… her mind raced on…in a never ending circle of doubt and despair. She knew she shouldn't have come.….snap out of it! She told herself…as she studied the structure…. slowly taking shape. It consumed her compelling her to continue driven, like some demonic designer. The devil certainly was in the details …She tried to throw a piece away…but the blood stuck to her…like some symbolic ritual? Blackfoot or Blood brothers? Perhaps RD could explain it to her…and if he couldn't? the cause, a cannibalistic coven.…craving for more? something so sinister feeding off her very thoughts? Fueling, fanning the flames? The more debaucherous the couple became the greater the opposing forces… of evil…vs good..like a renown rematch prize fight?

They'd soon be at each other's throats she feared; but why? for what reason?...she'd rather not go there!...Roxy quickly averted her gaze momentarily from the mausoleum like monstrosity that mimicked the historic landmark. Now their home, a horrible haunting foreboding feeling.... Out of the corner of her eye she spotted a large package of green tea...perfect thing to calm her nerves...take her mind off the lingering ludicrous thoughts of death and bloody sacrifices....and to lower her husband's blood pressure..He'd likely have a heart attack if her libido remained unchecked ...and ran rampant, out of control

"I'll likely do him in..if he's lucky!" she laughed in a hideous terrifying tone. She carefully prepared the tea...set the large vessel on the stove to boil...a bathtub full, for the enticing elixir. Roxy intuitively rummaged through the boxes, her digits seemed to return intermittently, or due to her dedication to the SAR mission, she didn't miss a thing. Her search ended as she discovered a box marked BONE CHINA. Inside, underneath several sheathes of thin woven cloth...like lens cleaner... lay buried a smashing set of what appeared to be authentic bone

china from the royal family themselves
perhaps…She peeled each individually wrapped
cup and saucer…getting another odd aura, a
sinister clairsentience just by touching and feeling
the surface of the tea service sets…she was
confused, stirred.. wondering if she was running a
fever?

"Am I coming down with something?' she
asked herself…. "An allergic reaction?"

The answer seemed reasonable enough. How
many hands had held the precious chalices? Dainty
digits, perhaps lady Diana herself?. damsels in
distress, trying to get away from the paparazzi,
stalkers, their lecherous husbands? Hideous
thoughts came over her again. She tried to erase
them from her mind by meticulous scrubbing of the
counters, the cups…her imagination runneth over
….with ridiculous ravaging and havoc wreaked
….where? she couldn't quite place the setting? As
her husband entered, she began to shake again
uncontrollably.

"You're a bundle of nerves" he quipped. His
medical history taking came to the fore, as he ran
through the questions, and corresponding

differential diagnoses in his mind. Possible causes of her case of the jitters; chill came to mind, obviously, attributable to her prancing about in nothing but a teddy or birthday suit. Which was still months away…but, the manuscript may take much longer than he anticipated at the rate of his repetitive outbursts…his bouts with the bottle would become more overbearing with each breath…and waking moment to mitigate the madness creeping into his mind. Uncontrollable rage….like a caged animal trying to claw it's way out. He ruled out tropical diseases, they hadn't been anywhere in a coon's age; but he'd heard of a tropical ear wick..that slowly burrowed it's way into the victim's grey matter via the ear canal, through the thin membrane of the ear drum… crawling around the semicircular canals…to decimate the host's sense of balance, then beeline straight for the brain via the auditory nerve; driving the poor devil mad, delirious, and ultimately driven to suicide! Had they been bitten by bed bugs? Or some form of mountain pine beetle? Roxy's madness may be attributable to Rocky Mountain fever…his definitely beaver fever! A host of high priority causes concerned him..perhaps a bad case of food poisoning? RD, the deceptively knowledgeable maintenance er rather medicine man, may be slipping something into their food? Their sea food sauces, a deadly tetrodotoxin?… Arsenic, the poison of choice for some of the nobility…Napolean did not notice 'til it was too late…his persistent stomach pains, caused by progressively greater doses of the drug of his wife's choosing. He had to snap out of it!

"Allergic…to life?" he chuckled. At the moment the comical suggestions actually seemed to be a reasonable response considering everything seemed to set her off. Perhaps it was something in the cleaning solutions? Or simply the inherent age of everything…Industrial disease dating back to the time of the coal mines and horse drawn carriages, the scourge of the lower cases. Perish the thought as he peered around the posh palace.

"Ever since we got here, you've been acting strange!"

She was awfully jumpy again…but before she could grab the large cleaver, he intercepted her intended trajectory and held her tight.

The water began to boil…the teapot sat a safe distance from the deep fryer…

Roxy released herself from his arms… as hers faded away…..he was satisfied she wouldn't harm herself. Roxy grabbed two tea cups by mind control it seemed, her limbs still missing in action; then poured the potent pain killer and mild laxative…She fumbled with the hot fluid and soon dropped the two saucers full of scalding hot tea…

"Damn it!" yelled her husband, concerned about running up quite a tab for their human errors. He oft declared stupidity kills….

As he picked up the sharp shards…he placed the pieces together to see if he could fix it…with a little crazy glue. Expecting to see MADE IN…… MINTON & CO., STOKE ON TRENT or other comparable reputable porcelain manufacturers. The fragments clearly spelled the phrase…

MADE IN WUTHERINGTON

"Odd"…Roxy looked at him thinking it was just a broken saucer… "didn't know they had a porcelain kiln nearby."

"Thank Thomas Frye" announced Roxy out of the blue. The renown inventor of soft porcelain paste in 1748, Bow China Works. Bone china referred to calcined cattle, that is animal bone ash that is used in porcelain and ceramics. He wasn't aware she was aware of how and where the ware was made. "inventing this fanciful form from which to indulge." She then made a mad dash in the direction of the deep fryer. He caught her in the nick of time, about to douse her digits…

"Cool it!" He subdued her, trying to calm her. She was definitely losing much more than her precious paws.

Dr Gum poured another cup of aromatic tea.

"Here, this will do you a world of good."

She wasn't so sure, skeptical…he smelled it… anticipating another aura.. a frightening feeling or clairsentience or fearsome fragrance - clairalience. But nothing novel enlightened her until the rim of the cup touched her lips…she dropped the coveted fragile chalice…it shattered into a million pieces on the tiled floor. Her pale complexion and demeanor startled him.. then in an acute case of paranoia she raised the point:

"Are you trying to poison me?" He was shocked by her statement. Something much more than skin deep had come over her…possessed?

Perhaps there was more substance to the native cards? He recalled the 'death' card, her pale complexion unnerved him…the sudden transition couldn't be explained by any natural phenomenon he rationalized. She was changing…for better or for worse, in sickness and in heath…he had to take her and the cards at face value… "But like of each thing that grows in season." (Shakespeare)

The happy honeymoon was turning into some preordained unfolding drama. The hotel may very well be a death trap to all who entered… a giant mousetrap, they the prisoners forced to run madly through the maze of hallways…and secret passageways like rats as long as they like or were permitted…By whom? RD?…he wasn't worried about the native warrior…what worried him most was…whatever was doing this…had made it's presence felt, known….the pesky ghosts? The mundane intermittent bottle rattling, and irritating trap door could all logically be explained by the brisk winds, and occasional gusts that crept through the cracks and orifices of the aging structure. Even the sudden power surge of the radio…could be ruled out as faulty wiring in the towering fire trap. The smoke from the 'peace pipe' proved more difficult to dispel. He hadn't found any trace of ash or cigar trailings in the ashtrays by his frequent visits to his favorite watering hole. Being the amateur detective and skeptical scientific investigator that he was, he wanted to know more about the inner working of what was going on in their minds…. a macabre mechanism seemed to have been set in motion the minute they walked through the front doors. Tripping a recurring prestaged performance? Perpetrated by the spirits? Or were they too, merely the pawns in this giant 3D chess match… yet where were the knights of old, the bishop? The rook? Albeit the residence with it's commanding view…gave the claimant naturally the title of 'king of the castle'.. his trusting queen by his side, in his kingdom, his realm or domain…He dwelt on the dilemma more deeply. There were still too many missing pieces. Perhaps insights into his 'peculair' penmanship may provide more answers? All in 'good' time? He wondered…good times, bad times Something was telling him this might simply be the appetizer in the apparition or entity's antics. He had all the time in the world to find out. Rome wasn't built in a day, neither was the POW. His wife's clever craftsmanship caught his eye…it reminded him of the hotel in every detail. He hadn't realized what hidden latent talents she had… Perhaps the hotel indeed did bring out the beast.. uh best in the both of them? Only time would tell. They'd have to wait and 'see', come what may…as he returned to erase the ridiculous bizarre words in big bold font. Something may be trying to tell him something? A message from the beyond? He took another swig from the soothing elixir to put a temporary stop to his insatiable curiosity. A check and balance….weighing his words carefully for good measure.

5: Culinary Delight

> "Cooking is like love. It should be
> entered into with abandon or not at
> all."
> - Harriet Van Horne

The disoriented dentist turned author was
abruptly awoken by the macabre jingling of bottles,
most empty as they rolled and banged about
against each other on the large black slab. He had
lost complete track of time as he forced his heavy
eyelids apart and laboriously raised his head.....He
shivered, famished, freezing; his frosty breath
coated the screen of his laptop. In stark contrast to
the dark pale shades of death that lingered in

disarray on the ebony wood, the panorama outside was a completely eye opening story all together. A winter wonderland as far as the eye could see. All around the hotel, on the hilltops, the frosty white 2' thick blanket rose high up into the step mountain valleys disappearing at the pinnacles, impossible to distinguish in the weird all encompassing pearly white hue. Had he died and gone to heaven he wondered. Such a sudden monumental magical transformation. RD indeed, true to his word, was nowhere to be found. He sought the company of his angelic assistant but couldn't determined her whereabouts. Was she playing a little game of hide and seek? Did the two disappear into his secret den hideaway for a romantic illicit tryst, tempted by the risk of discovery? He wandered through the hotel ...woozy, wondering where everyone had gone. Bleary eyed, he bumped into several walls... There were too many hallways, he'd likely get lost....and freeze to death up there some where like a homeless vagrant camping out in the cavernous enclosure. He decided to venture into the gargantuan galley and dug up some grub on his own before he passed out from lack of fuel.

"Food is an important part of a balanced diet" harped his wife continually. Where was she? He missed her already, her allure added measures to the ambience of their humble abode. "My wife dresses to kill. She cooks that way too." (Henny Youngman) He chuckled…and caught the elevator. It took an eternity, trapped in the small cage…he'd likely starve to death by the time it reached the ground floor, he felt like some long forgotten Minah bird or pet parrot. Yet it was the sound of her sweet voice mimicking everything she read; he missed. He finally found his bearings, the booze becoming a beast of burden…as he banged against the long cold steel counter. He tried to focus on the ingredients strewn all over, the flour and the miniature POW replica off in the distance unnerved him thinking he'd wandered in his sleep outside…walking about..bound to fall asleep and slowly freeze to death. Such a stupid mistake… what was going on? He had to get a grip as he gazed around the galley; recognizing the chef's hat, he grabbed it, then pushed it down over his

throbbing head. Instinctively he grabbed a
sharp cleaver. This wasn't rocket science, he
realized, his dexterity and concentration slowly
came back to him,

"Can't be that difficult? If I can master surgery,
the culinary arts must be child's play." He focused
intensely on the recipes - rather precise formulas
like former organic chemistry or biochemistry
experiments, he meticulously measured in
miniscule amounts then extrapolated for larger
feasts. Like a learned alchemist or distiller he
methodically mixed the test samples, tasting…a
little dash here or pinch of potent spice there. He
began to assemble the dishes. The first item he
figured, finger food…, the dainty 'lady fingers'.
Beating the eggs, sugar and flour.. feeling for the
'spongy' texture, he began to arrange them,
imagining Roxy's hands as a guide…as he placed
his on the flour….he arranged several rows of hand
prints…then baptized them in the bowls. He'd
emptied several bottles of 80 proof rum in lieu of
vanilla extract and let them bath and marinate in
the aromatic bath. A yummy yucca flux? He
dunked the digits…declaring:

"I christen thee lady Godiva…no Chatter….ly…albeit he desperately sought her soft mimicry …most of the time she was the listener, lapping up his lengthy lectures.

He kept sampling the sweet savory 'strong' super saturated sauce well on his way to getting soused. The alluring aroma of apricots, peaches and other exotic fruits of the deceptively potent potion, sufficient for a TKO- the knock out punch!

 The chef considered the 2nd round of the 1st course. An entree, a soup? 'Black Eyed Peas' to ring in a prosperous year of good luck and future fortunes came to mind, mind you new year's eve was still a 2 months away. Why not? He prepared the tiny 'eyes'; the booze beginning to cloud his concentration, he began to imagine an eyeball, then another, and another, soon an entire audience stared back up at him, all eyes fixed on his every move. His former classmates in the operating theater? Or the fans waiting to devour his diabolical thriller. The pressure of producing and penning a best seller was getting to him.

 "Gotta get a grip!" as he pondered the main course…casserole? Pot luck style..perusing the shelves for random ingredients.. Black eyed peas, mushroom soup, crushed potatoe chips, tuna or salmon…He tore into a bag of chips…then poured the contents onto the counter to crush them. The crumbly wafers became fragile floppy ear lobe cartilages…he crushed them with the meat tenderizer.. mumbling to himself…as if hanging, clinging onto his every word. He stopped reassured by the silence. He was losing his mind. He opened the can of mushroom soup…with some difficulty then realized…

"Did I open the right can?" A chill came over him as he imagined countless knobs…artichokes?

"Tiny Buffalo hearts? What did RD mention? Best served fresh?" thumping, beating, all in unison, he tossed a handful of the helpless transplant donors onto the cutting board…then maniacally sliced and diced them into slivers in a futile attempt to silence them. He didn't want to leave a trace…something came over him… …a sinister sensation.

"Man is the only animal that can remain on friendly terms with the victims he intends to eat ….until he eats them." (Samuel Butler)

He found a slimy scaly fish still dripping and filleted it, crushing the bony spine and all then stuffed it into the casserole dish… into it he added all the other spare 'parts'…He took globs of the gooey ingredients, kneading, working feverishly to make a rancid wretched sloppy dough. Stuffing it into the pyrex dish, he molded the mass into two mounds …like two hemispheres of a human brain splitting the centerline, the central sulcus of the corpus callosum, perhaps massive mammaries or sweet butt cheeks? He smiled, satisfied with his handiwork…and ripped a sheet of aluminum, crimped the edges carefully then shoved it into the oven. His 'chirgeon' culinary craft was coming along nicely, then decided on the next dish. Liver and onions, a delicacy if done right. He approached the clear compartments; they wreaked. A power outage? Perhaps Roxy had carelessly left the door open, perish the thought, he'd trained his assistant well. Why the trail of blood, dripping from the… fresh venison..of course! He slammed the lobes of liver onto the slab, imagining a life threatening liver transplant he believed the booze brought about the 'vision'…He drowned his efforts by

dousing the dismembered sections adding a
dash of spices and garnish then shoved them into
the gaping hot orifice.

He approached the potatoes, slowly, cautiously,
then carefully peeled a thin continuous millimeter
thick unwinding peel..like a sensitive skin graft
….beginner's luck or a lengthy career…grafting
the burn victims?..he knew not which? Sufficient
to stuff a body suit…the peels, like miles of
cellulose of film footage, filled the cutting room of
the editing suite. He flipped the film onto several
pans, patted it down …

"A little more marinade?"

He reached for a bottle of grand marnier…from
the collection, the secret ingredients to the cunning
colonel's culinary delight? He was unaware of the
serious danger of igniting the entire galley…by the
clutter of bottles clanging on the counter. About to
light the Olympic Torch? The flambé bound to
erupt in an all encompassing explosion….Some
thing caught his attention out of the corner of
his eye on the fresh fallen snow. In his inebriated
state he imagined his feisty wife, the rambunctious
deer, frolicking about in the winter wonder

land, giving him the slip. He dashed to the window…and peered at the trail of small hoof prints…deer? Antelope? His gazelle, Lady Godiva at play? His snow angel, au naturele? He slipped deeper into a drunken stupor…delirious desiring his damsel…in distress? He didn't know the difference at this point…no matter, they'd all shed their skin and emerge as beautiful butterflies in the spring anyway! He performed a makeshift triage with tight tourniquets, wrapping and twisting several 'dogs in blankets'.. then tossed them hurriedly into the hot blast furnace. He couldn't distinguish between saving lives or dismembering them, at this stage. Why he couldn't remember how he even got into this mess in the first place.. as he peered around his elaborate embalming chamber. He thought long and hard about the last course..

"Dessert is probably the most important part of the meal, since it will be the last thing your guests remember before they pass out all over the table." (The Anarchist Cookbook)

"Hmmm….death by chocolate." He was too drunk to activate, let alone find the chocolate

fountain or the fondue pot. Instead by dumb
blind luck, intuitively turned on the deep fryer. He
visualized a variant of the 'awesome blossom'
or 'bloomin' onion'…then rushed to the fridge.
There he found a large head of cabbage..about the
size of his wife's head. He placed two 'black eyed
peas' near where he imagined the windows to her
soul were. He dissected two narrow sluiceways, in
lieu of any ears of corn, he jammed two potatoe
chips on either side of the gruesome growing
grimace. The caricaturist quickly cracked a carrot
in two, then stuck the end into the lettuce folds to
form a pudgy nose. With one sift swoop he brought
the razor sharp blade to bear down on the bright
red hot chili pepper. It split in two…delicately, he
inserted the slices, supposedly her sizzling luscious
ruby red lips. He licked the face of 'mrs potatoe
head' hedonistically. Satisfied, without a care, he
tossed the curious caricature into the deep fryer.
The oil began to splatter all over like a stormy sea..
the imminent threat of kindling an aging dry cloth
napkin did not seem to phase him. He peered
around to finalize the arrangements. The finishing
touches to a small romantic table for two near the

window of the Stallworthy Dining room. He found some red roses...silk or fresh, did not seem to dissuade him. He sliced the ends off the long stems. In lieu of a vase, presumably still packed amongst all the other fine crystal, he popped them into a plastic 'Budweiser' beer jug, left by the staff he assumed, and placed it on the table. Dinner ware? Or where oh where can it be? He raised his cleaver and chopped the end off the cardboard box marked 'fine porcelain bone china' like an executioner, swift to deliberate and deliver the fatal death blow. He ripped the cardboard, then brought a few plates in front of his nose, in a futile attempt to bring them into focus.

"Hmm, rather heavy" he slurred.. startled by the rather large cumbersome 'frisbees'. He lined up several bottles, deceptively doubling in his blurred vision, precariously perched on the counter next to the deep fryer... He cocked his arm then flung the flying objects in the general direction of the bowling alley assembly of glass pins. Like a gattling gun, or rattling saber, the projectile sliced the necks off several bottles, shattering into several shards like a skeet shot that had found it's target.

The alcohol dripped ominously over the counter…inches away for the deep fryer definitely a bad omen! He hoisted a broken bottle, a toast to his multi talented accomplishment, and inspite of the monumental macabre mess, he may have pulled off the POW dinner party of decade? He let the delicious drops of liquor fall onto his tongue.. the sharp edges of the broken glass only inches away from his tantalized taste buds. The decadent postnuptial preparations…albeit an eyesore, did deliver a powerful statement…that the chef's resourceful undertaking not be underestimated or taken for granted. Something had definitely gotten a hold of him….the persistent recurring ghosts of the hotel's haunted past? Or future foreboding spirits yet to reveal themselves? The two made quite a couple he cheered. His clever culinary concoctions certainly equaled her architectural arrangements as he eyed the eerie miniature replica of the POW. What deep dark delicious secrets lay inside he wondered?

"I've got to hand it to her…" as he stepped closer to examine the intricate craftsmanship. His bleary vision…couldn't discern the details…nor notice the trail of blood oozing from the features…seeping in unison with the sinister escalating events unfolding inside the actual architectural treasure?

He rubbed his hands…excitedly…

"Dinner is served." He stumbled and tripped nearly flattening his face against the scorching surface of the inferno inside the oven. The heat was unbearable, he had to get out…As he turned toward the picturesque panorama outside, he noticed several shadowy figures around him in the reflection of the frosty window pane.

"Well, well… looks like we have a full house. Guess whoooo's coming?"…he turned around but saw that he was the lone solitary sous chef out standing in his field of shattered dreams.

"Huh?"

No one materialized in the massive mansion. He peered around the empty void; were all his plans in vain? He walked toward the lobby, equally eerily still. Had they abandoned him? Left him in solitary confinement, a prisoner of his own device, and evil depraved vices? He saw a faint outline near his desk…an apparition ..a rather wretched looking ghost writer, Isaac Asimov? Typing madly in a frenzy…when asked 'if he had to do it all over again?… he'd remarked, I'd type faster!'

"RD, is that you? My ghost writer….nothing runs like a deer." He chuckled.. yet in the back of his mind, he knew he was cracking up, going crazy…by simply being here….the hotel was slowly getting to him….he preferred that Roxy found him first…where was his elusive enchanting creature? He turned to peer out into the white canvas that rapidly receded into utter darkness beyond the boundary of the POW's perimeter lighting and the steep drop off down to the icy lake level. He spotted a ghostly figure.. then quickly turned around…disappointed by the lifeless white sheets still draped over some of the luxurious high back leather chairs…curiously he had to make sure she wasn't hiding, cowering underneath. He peeled the cold sheets back …hoping to find his delectable damsel, distraught and utterly disappointed at the no show, his clandestine dinner date had deserted him. He decided to drown his sorrows with each and every entoxicating elixir he could name. He'd cry a river of tears in the Weeping Willow before daybreak he figured. He shuffled toward the stained glass doorway as if engaged in a funeral march mesmerized in a daze, gloomily he hung his head as if going off to the gallows pole. His heart suddenly leapt as he caught a glimpse of a strange black and white form, a feathery plumage, an odd ostrich roaming the residence...the preferred pet of the nobility? It gave him quite a fright. He tried to focus. Two long statuesque legs came into his field of vision, not the spindly sticks of the flightless bird, but full round figures projecting from the massive black and white folds.

"Roxy, is that you? The deer and antelope at play?" Indeed, it was the sly seductive creature, in a sexy French maid outfit, ostrich feather duster in hand, near the gift shop, tickling the trinkets and large bulbous protrusion at the onset of the of the ornate oak handrail. He rubbed his eyes in disbelief stumbling over the stained glass door riser.

"You hooooo, catch me if you can!" echoed enticingly throughout the empty acoustic chamber. He crashed into several glass shelves like a bull in a china shop chasing her elusive ghostly form into the gift shop. He emerged bleeding, riled, hot on

her trail. He looked up into the loft lobby…
alongside the balcony on the third floor, she
delicately dusted the accumulation of debris..that
formed a feathery light cloud in the central hiatus
of the hotel.

"You can do better than that!" she declared,
"Come on", intent on luring the savage beast into
her private boudoir. He dropped down on all fours
like an enraged wolf or grizzly bear, then rushed
toward her last lingering utterance. He propped
himself up on his hind haunches, then sniffed the
stale filthy cloud that descended on top of him.
Nano particles of her intoxicating perfume
permeated his nostrils, the miscible mixture made
him mad with desire. He nearly ripped the door off
the elevator cage, then hurried inside. He ambled
around inside the confining enclosure like a
creature gone wild. He waited an eternity before it
arrived at it's destination on the 4th. He desperately
needed another drink as he left a slobbery trail
along the hallway.

"Yoo hoo" emanated from the end of the
hallway. His eyes darted to his left and right, to
orient himself in the direction of the source of the

sound. He spotted a small plumage, no bigger than a turkey or pheasant, then sprang toward it, nearly plunging to his death as he grabbed the feather duster and tore it apart. He flung himself back off the solid oak balcony and took a deep breath…It was close, too close for comfort. His tempting target was still well out of reach as she rushed into the upper ramparts. From the depths of a 5th floor balcony he heard a heavenly voice,

"Hurry up, I'll be waiting!"

He hustled to the narrow stairwell, still sloshed and extremely unstable…

"OK, focus, you can do this" he urged himself reaching out shaking in vain to grip the rail…he clawed the air frantically and finally found the dusty hand rail. He watched his feet slowly ascend the steep steps…

"That's it, one foot after another." He slowly crept up the narrow passageway in pursuit of his prey.

"Come on, you old bear." Came the reply, egging him on. Shedding her skin, he found another article of outer wear…a vivacious Victoria Secret black and white maid's outfit.

"Bear, my ass." He steamed, miffed by her provocative foreplay. He knew he'd find her..she was running out of real estate up on the sixth floor. He turned to his left then right…she'd left her white lingerie draped over the rail…to lead him on. He bolted toward the bra and panties beacon like a moth to a flame…he stopped to listen for a sound but she was much too smart to give away her position. He mounted the step ladder like steps then found another large mass, the large frilly fluffy white plumage…the last of her clever decoy camouflage. It was down to a few dimly lit dens and deceptive passageways. He recognized her faint outline..near the open trap door…overcome with fright. He dreaded another death defying descent, a fatal reenactment, and fall to her death by his beloved..

"Roxy, nooooo!"

He reached out and grabbed what looked like the last feather…and in so doing, sealed his own fate as he lost his balance, about to take a deadly tumble. Luckily a gust of wind or an instinctive gut reaction slammed the trap door shut. He dropped like a dead weight on top of the impediment and bore the brunt of the fall with his forehead. Dazed and confused he looked up and saw a pale faced angelic apparition above him.

"Roxy?"

He raised his sore head, leaning forward, his parched lips yearned for a taste of her tantalizing sweet nectar…just out of reach. He saw the image of a naked nymh..her arm reached around the edge of a corridor…then lost his balance, fell back and slammed his head on the barrier. He lost his consciousness in the process. An eternity may have passed before he awoke…cold, confused..shaken and stirred by the last lingering images. There were no traces of the piles of discarded apparel. He hurried back to the Lakeview Suite, certain she'd be waiting there for him spread out on the satin sheets au naturelle…

"Honey, I'm home." He dejectedly discovered the bare room and ensuite. No sign of goldilocks, not a chocolate upon the pillows nor even a note. The grumpy bear left the den disgruntled, snorting in disgust like a deprived animal in heat. Halfway down the hall he detected smoke..coming from the kitchen? How long he'd left his baking drew a complete blank. 'Smokey the bear' bolted down the stairs, blazing a trail, beelining for the source of the smoke. You'd never seen a bear move so fast! He arrived in the nick of time as his wife doused the flames...in slinky sexy evening wear.. where had the time flown? She grabbed the bubbling boiling pyrex dishes and pans from the inferno with the large webbed oven kevlar nomex mitts, then arranged the assortment of tantalizing entrees along the counter...The most appetizing dish, an alluring two legged treat stood right before his bleary eyes. It brought him back to an acute conscious state of awareness.

"Surprise! I prepared some of your favorite dishes" he presumed, at least taken a stab at it. "Here let me" as he urged her to take it easy and a load off her feet after the fanciful frolic and free for all up in the nose bleed section of the balconies.

"Why don't you take a window seat?" The knotty wooden 'reserved' sign and Bud pitcher took the event over the top and kicked it up a notch. She was pleasantly surprised by his tenacious attempt to please her...yet preferred to do the cooking. She didn't dare let him get too distracted and dilute his talents…albeit as she noticed the disarray of broken bottles, she feared the worst. What the h…had gone on in here, she wondered… examining the virtual ravaged war zone.

RD came rushing into the kitchen from the neighboring building via the back exit. He couldn't believe it was completely kaput! lying in utter ruin as if the cooks had rioted, retaliated over a pay cut or firing.

"Everything alright? I thought I smelled smoke."

"Sure it wasn't your ghost, and his ghastly cigar aroma?" The stench was overwhelming…Roxy had salvaged most of the entrees…

"Everything's fine" she assured RD; she hurried him out..so the two could share in a moment of culinary delight all to themselves.

RD was relieved and returned from whence he came…to get a good night's rest. Roxy was lost in thought…pondering the deceptively dangerous deep fresh fallen snow. It made travel next to impossible inside the park. They were literally trapped now…prisoners of the POW for the duration of the winter. No way in and no way out….she feared they'd run out of food well before spring as she scoured the ruins. Shattered shards of glass, porcelain plates, precious souvenirs and reminders of the past? She tried to blot out the battle scene and focused on a brighter future, and better times ahead as her husband brought the first heaping tray of decadent appetizers. Still donning the chef's hat, she laughed at the buffoon.

The fingers floated like river rafts, or drift wood adjacent to one another slowly separating, steeped in the savory 80 proof sauce…of liqueurs and brandies…

"So many fingers" remarked Roxy, rather alarmed. The plate of peculiar polydactylism upset her as she touched one of the digits. An aura of clairalience and clairsentience followed by an acute panic attack tipped her over the edge. She took one bite of the crunchy finger and almost immediately was repulsed by the brittle bone crunching sound and hideous implication and possibility she'd noshed on a real human finger. Saved only by the supersaturated alcoholic sauce to assuage her fear and feelings of fright…she rapidly succumbed to the pleasant anaesthetic effect of the alcohol.

It dulled her senses…sending her drifting off in a decadent dreamy state of disbelief and suspended animation.

"Ah, the lettuce"..reminded the respected clinician, his culinary skills needed refinement.

He removed the gruesome head, which had shrunk like a cannibalized specimen rather than grew some more. He quickly slid and concealed it under a silver platter.

"Let us pray!" urged Roxy…as she lowered her head…and placed her hands together on her lap. He set the platter on the table and hurriedly mirrored her posture on his side of the table…both bowed in prayer.

"Bless us in the midst of all the turmoil…" She dared not open an eye to peer about the ruins. "…. in the world today. Lord, grant us a blessed stay, keep us safe; provide the inspiration for provocative penmanship…and deliver us from evil." The short but all encompassing request seemed like a prelude to what she felt may be in store for them…particularly the emphasis on evil.

"Amen" they repeated in unison sitting together for the first time since arriving…

"Before we begin" as he hoisted his glass…
"may we exit this year reflecting on all the good
fortune to fall in our laps…and be truly blessed in
the coming new year."

Their glasses clang as they shared an intimate
moment. Her festive mood soon turned to sheer
terror as she continued to see sordid body parts
as he presented each entrée. The beady black eyed
peas ogled her like the prying eyes of the paparazzi
bobbing up and down in the blood colored broth.
She nearly brought up her breakfast…repulsed by
the vision.

"Not eating your soup? This place is tapping
your strength." As she lifted the lid on the
casserole dish she shuddered shocked by the sight
of the severed section of grey matter or more
macabre rump roast?.. the atrocious anatomical
depictions left little doubt, her husband was trying
to drive her mad. How could he? He knew her
disdain for his distinct dental training…deserved
some degree of elucidation.

"Full moon? Take it away!" she demanded. He
quickly removed his creations. Each tray repulsed
her more…the artichokes like small sliced hearts

had her in an uproar…all she saw was blood and ghastly remnants of a viciously dismembered human being…perhaps one of his college pranks? She thought he'd ceased his shenanigans. All the demons of his past seemed to be resurfacing.

"Honey, are you alright?"

As a last resort she sampled the wrapped meat, presumably 'pigs in blankets'? She was utterly repulsed by what seemed like severed penises …what pray tell was he thinking?

She tossed her napkin on top of the macabre suggestive trays…thoroughly disgusted, then stormed from the table.

"Aren't you staying for dessert?" he questioned

"Let go of me you cunning culinary linguist …trying to talk me into…."

"But" he pauses pleading his case. "Give me another chance, I'm not Wolfgang Puck."

"No, you're a f…k up!" the fool, the tarot prediction coming to the fore?

6: Cabin Fever

"Adversity causes some men to break,
others to break records."
- William Ward

Roxy screamed; ere she fled, caught a glimpse
of her baked pride and joy, the POW replica now
oozed a continuous thick stream of bloody red
exudate from every orifice as if flowing from a
hospital inundated with victims of a fatal
hemorrhagic fever infection. She sensed her own
finiteness in a forthcoming fatal tragic end
….as she raced out the front entrance through the

lobby. Roxy broke out into a sweat. Every second counted, every decision she'd make now conceivably her last…a million options clouded her over taxed muddled mind. The alcohol had effectively mitigated her split second decision making ability, rendering it practically impossible to think straight. As a result, her erratic random motion, bumping into the front desk….banging on the front desk bell in desperation…only drove her more crazy. The ringing like the tintinnabulation of bell's, her death knell, left her at a loss. She bent down to grab her ailing ankle, she'd somehow twisted it on the way out the door. She caught a glimpse of her crazed assailant and her second wind. In desperation, a last ditch effort, she chose the stairs. The elevator cage she knew spelled certain death, like entering the chamber at the end of the green mile, a death sentence. Her only chance to evade her captor, confused her in the endless array of rooms and hallways and dead ends. She'd rather leap to her death from an upper floor balcony, driven to suicide like all the other unfortunate predecessors, than face her maker, her husband? Why his radical departure from reality, she knew not, it made no sense at all! She had neither the time to formulate nor venture a guess.. as she clawed her way up the stairs… her daily jogging routine would serve her well she figured. She placed her chances at outrunning her hunter at 50:50 provided she did not run out of real estate. ….A deadly game of hide and seek commenced. Her primal fear nagged her, knowing she may have to resort to 'hiding out' in a dark confining recess somewhere within the walls of the withering, eroding edifice. Play the waiting game, certain to die of starvation or slowly succumb to something much more sinister she felt lurked deep within the structure. She was sure of it. Somehow it had affected her husband's sanity, sense of self, his awareness now completely clouded by the continuous imbibing of the potent tempting toxic elixir…A Christmas she'd never forget, provided she witnessed the advent of the approaching holiday alive. "What do you call people afraid of Santa Claus? Claustrophobic. She giggled hysterically like a giddy school girl, giving away her location. Her husband peered up into the vast expanse eyeing the trap door. The macabre demeanor and crazed look on his face, a foreboding frightening revelation. Any remnant of his former normal self, the ethical moral medical professional, now lost somewhere in the lofty ramparts. "I want to lobby for God" (Billy Graham) he yelled…then called out to her. He burst into a hideous cackle…certain he'd soon catch his petrified prey. The only obstacle that lay between him and his elusive target were the towering hewn timbers that demarcated the intricate maze of the magnificent monument. It had certainly seen better days; dramatic displays of dance, music and elegant decorum appreciated by a much more distinguished audience. This evening, certain to end in a Greek tragedy, or vicious brutal murder, made no sense whatsoever. What had come over the aspiring author; losing all inhibitions and sense of human decency. His depravity and wanton desires driven by the devil himself, would soon be fulfilled he felt. From where the urges came, he knew not. The incessant impulse to fulfill the preordained prophecy…the chaos and the death card drove him mad. Roxy's deeply rooted fears fueled by the rumors of the former ghosts and goblins also faded. "I'm not afraid of werewolves or vampires or haunted hotels, I'm afraid of what real human beings do to other real human beings." (Walter Williams). Her subconscious aversion to accepting the demonic forces that now seemed to rule the regal residence surfaced. It ran amuck with her vivid imagination. Coupled by the prospect of being beaten to a pulp or chopped into a fine garnish for her husband's ghoulash... left her with a hideous realization....that she'd run into the ultimate evil personified sooner or later. She felt he was strong enough to purge the demons that drove him to wantonly commit such a terrifying feat....but where would they surface...prey upon the only other resident? And where was Running Deer in the midst of this madness? perhaps he had seen the performance before, over and over, the passion play that ultimately drove the tenants, the brief travelers in time, to utter ruin.. and probably their deaths. How or why she wondered as she quietly snuck her way down each dimly lit corridor. Her acute sense of hearing, perhaps part clairaudience, or clear hearing, contributed to her confidence, and escalated her chance of escape. She heard the drunken fool fumble his way, slobbery like a rabid animal run round and round in circles. He was thoroughly confused and lost in the long linear hallways. His blurred vision and obliterated powers of logic and reason, could not shed light on the same set of doors and rooms that he continued to repeatedly pass, they were clearly numbered. Perhaps another ploy by the apparitions in his altered state of awareness? Leading him, urging him on, having lost all sense of direction or desire to contain his craving to kill her. He could not see the forest from the trees nor distinguish his frightened spouse standing perfectly still from a totem pole. His young bride refrained from returning to the honeymoon suite. 321..the final chilling countdown? The honeymoon for all intents and purposes by all accounts was over.

"...can't go back to the room... 1st place he'll look!" she feared. She recalled the floor plan from the front desk...from a few days ago... 86 rooms... the haunted room 512, only available upon request. She hoped the number would remain at that tolerable total. Yet the persistent fear of becoming

a statistic haunted her. A hellish horrific end
….Not if I kill him first she mulled over in her
mind…where there was a will…she wondered if he
had even included her in his will; probably penned
out permanently in the prenuptial rush. There must
be a way out of this nightmare. Roxy raced around
a corner and came upon a glass case housing a
foam fire extinguisher and axe. She had no axe to
grind with her husband, the gregarious generous
giver.. yet knew deep down in her gut, that if she
did not defend herself, she'd be gutted, filleted and
served for dinner by the dentist turned demented
chef! The throbbing pain in her chest grew…more
intense than the worst case of heartburn…She
ripped a section of her slinky dinner dress and
wrapped it around her wrist careful not to cut
herself and potentially bleed to death. She wouldn't
allow it. Neither the hotel nor the mini macabre
replica would claim her.

"It was Elvis who really got me hooked on beat
music. When I heard 'Heartbreak Hotel', that was
it." (Paul McCartney) counting down…three, two,
one….then smashed the glass. She greedily
grabbed the heavy hatchet from the 'dispenser'..

Luckily the lunatic was lost in a hallway diametrically opposed to hers. He'd run round and round…reaching the end of his wits and runways several times…beating his head against the thick doors, never once stopping to or simply bother to read the room numbers. Was this the end? He'd driven himself mad, insane, incessantly ranting and raving…Roxy….his hideous howls, and yelps left her unhinged. Her only hope…distance herself as far as she could short of climbing up into the bell tower turret and freeze to death. They'd find her frozen body in the spring she figured, or served to the wolves to satisfy their hideous howling. They seemed to sense the sinister situation which she faced, intuitively.

Suddenly the loud boisterous belligerent outbursts ceased. Had he fallen asleep or slipped and fallen, unable to get up? Had he finally come to his senses? She trembled and waited an eternity. Had the soused slob had a change of heart, and made a decisive u turn… near the stairs… He descended with the conviction of a devil make care demented maniac…

"Hmmm…death by chocolate…" the words

reverberated over and over again in his mind. Such a decadent way to die...he raced through the lobby to implement his prescription for murder. He set all the burners on full boil.. to prepare the powerful soothing potion; in other words, prepare the boiling oil and chocolate concoction, equal parts he calculated....certain to heat and retain the luxurious emollients....He heaved several large pots onto the scorching elements breaking out into a sweat from the exhaustive work. The strenuous workout might do him a world of good he figured as he waited for the water to come to a boil. In lieu of a large fiesty lobster, he'd boil a much larger two legged female of the species. He scoured the galley for a reliable method to haul the heavy load to the honeymoon suite. The beast of burden...

In a flash, he found the tempting tea cart...from which she had taunted and teased him so effectively. It was his turn to return the favor..with a flavorful baptismal font filled with her favorite flavor. The first 'pot luck' or pot of luxurious oils and chocolate mixture was coming to a boil. All the bubbling cauldron required now was one seasoned hallowed witch to recite an appropriate incantation.

In lieu of the latter he'd perform the honors. He hurriedly slid the beast, the bubbling bath water, onto the tray. The top heavy contents swayed on the rickety albeit surprisingly resilient 4 wheeled roller. Her luck was slowly running out it seemed as he rushed his personal interpretation of 'room service' into the elevator. He hurriedly stepped out and laboriously pushed the cart toward the room, 321…

"Oh Rock seee… I have a surprise for you…" She heard his wretched voice and knew at once she had made the correct choice in the macabre multiple choice game. She trembled in the dark corner. The alcohol had gone to her head and slowly knocked out her state of wakefulness. She knew she couldn't fall asleep as she clutched the weapon of choice. An imminent duel to the death may settle the score and end this bizarre nightmare once and for all. She had to be wide awake or suffer the consequences of their animalistic actions.

Inside the ensuite he poured the contents of the vessel into the deep basin. The hot oil and chocolate mixture splashed all over the room. He had to quickly return to the galley to fill 'er up and preserve the precious heat…In a series of successive heaves and vaulting motions that demanded superhuman strength, like that of a caber tosser, he accomplished his task.. The dedicated dentist had never failed to fulfill a goal once set in motion in his mind. He moved the next vessel into place next to the bath. It topped up the receptacle nicely…allowing the entire torso of his beloved wife to be completely dunked, double dipped, doused, immersed, baptized. A ludicrous wide grin spread across his face. The hideous laugh that accompanied the grimace could wake the dead. It luckily stirred his scared wife…battling to stay wide awake in the event of a close encounter of the worst kind. 'death is someone you see very clearly with eyes in the center of your heart: eyes that see not by reacting to light but by reacting to a kind of chill from within the marrow of your own life." (Thomas Merton) He left the room and reached the balcony, to announce his plan to alleviate her tension.

"Oh Rocksee dear…I've drawn your favorite

bubble bath… just like you like it… nice and chocolatey…and oh so hawwwwwwwwt."

The announcement echoed through the lobby. It left a lingering low level reverberation that could be felt down to the foyer. Perhaps a simultaneous icy drafty gust from an open window gave the words flight. He fought his own demons, desperate to remain conscious. The alcoholic concoctions had worn down his inhibitions as he sought to resourcefully remedy her aching muscles. Yet they had also taken a toll on his sense of time and space. How many trips he had made back and forth to the room, certainly a respectable room service record, showed complete disdain and disrespect for her wishes. His metabolic rate, as a result of all the strenuous exertion, was raised through the roof. The rapid irregular heart beat…made him dizzy..as he leaned over the balcony rail…peering blankly off into space.. to seek his prey. The dramatic turn of events from the time they said grace at the dinner table to this enlightening end to a long day did not seem to disturb him. The thought that a demonic spirit other than his own spirited indulgence was responsible for the rather erratic

out of character charade did not cross his
mind. He prepared to fulfill his promise, to provide
her with a lasting memory. His prescription to
allow her to slip into sweet slumber..unfortunately
unbeknownst to him....likely forever. The lovely
long lingering bath...that was certain to unsettle
her to her very marrow's core.

She stirred and desperately sought to shake off
the incessant craving to drift off into utter
unconsciousness, ultimately sealing her fate. She
fought feverishly....suddenly, she heard her
husband's harsh voice, it's deep dull demonic
rumble resulted in an immediate acceleration of her
heart rate. She trembled....breaking out into
another persistent sweat....equivalent to an entire
morning's run she estimated. The enormous
expenditure of energy excited her in the transitory
state between total intoxication and an intense
physical workout. Like a near death experience,
(NDE) she teetered in the netherlands of her mind;
the grey zone...perhaps she was already dying she
fretted...He may have already dealt the fatal blow,
and let her slowly bleed to death like a discarded
dish rag? She ran her trembling fingers over her

body…but could not distinguish between blood and sweat…like the last moments of Christ's life as his vital bodily fluids flowed from his gaping stab wounds mixed with the bitter sweet vinagrette that the Roman soldiers doused his forehead with. She'd give her soul to be anywhere else but here…in this unholy hellish haven. But the world itself was within reach of the raving lunatic…he'd likely track her to the ends of the earth to execute his prescription to persecute and prosecute her. Such a trivial pursuit she reasoned, how had she ever put herself in this predicament? A simple yes, consenting to the clandestine, prearranged getaway. Such a fatal blunder she fretted. The macabre premeditated meeting had so much more than meets the eye….suddenly out of the corner of her eye she caught a glimpse of the garish grimace. The raving lunatic sniffed the air….sensing the scent of a woman…his other half of flesh and blood cowering in the dark corner ….She could not contain herself and emitted a short deep sigh of sheer terror. He turned.. like a crazy caveman who'd honed his hunting skills…in pursuit of his prey knowing that an uneventful outing could lead to his demise and the end of his clan, lineage, and perhaps the extinction of the entire human species. Inspite of the surge of adrenaline that had coursed throughout her veins, her body suddenly ceased to respond to her plea to perform it's basic functions....she nodded off...not knowing now whether she'd live or die....and drifted off into sweet slumber....immediately she was elevated...up above the clouds from the lofty perspective....seeming to float far above the rugged mountainous terrain... she did not fight the peaceful serene feeling...but let it envelop her completely. She did not recognize the region....nor was there an apparent itinerary anywhere within reach or sight...in fact she did not detect any in flight features...no cramped confining seats in front of her...her sore feet were free to stretch out...in a totally prone position, the amazing leg room, perhaps it was a new novel Virgin variant of first class travel...she peered to one side but was startled by the fact there was no one else flying with her.. or onboard....the small porthole was also completely transparent or apparently not there at all.... she simply soared high above the clouds...as if carried off to a mysterious marvelous destination. She enjoyed the silence, the tranquility …and let the mystifying dream take it's course …the clouds slowly dissipated.. her attitude rapidly transformed as she sensed her altitude rapidly decrease, in fact, she felt a decent at a pronounced pace…. Like a cruise missile zooming toward it's intended target….she felt as if she were being drawn out of the protective enclosure….as if being sucked out of the sealed cabin enclosure, perhaps a fatal accident enroute had occurred? Pilot error? Perish the thought…but the persistent ominous premonition or presumably live transmission refused to let her escape…During the rapid descent she slowly began to recognize the surrounding terrain….certainly nowhere near a known runway or landing strip. She was not warned to fasten her seat belts on a dramatic final approach…in fact no flight crew could be found anywhere within her perspective….Roxy's rapid heart beat resumed ….pounding inside her chest. Copious amounts of perspiration in anticipation of a fatal crash fell from her forehead….she could not close her eyes or shut out the inevitable…the end in sight?…She desperately sought a way out of her nightmare that now rivaled her previous predicament..but she was forced to endure the entire episode wide awake. Roxy had never suffered a nervous bout aboard an airliner, she had no fear of flying that she knew of. Yet the complete lack of control in her fall confused her. She had read that anyone who falls to their death from a cliff or any lofty height is oft pronounced dead…never waking from their vivid lucid dream. She fought feverishly to wake from the weird surreal sensation…. To compound the problem she suddenly recognized a horrific landmark. It can't be…NO…She refused to open her eyes yet the recurring image shocked her to her very soul…. the satellite like image of the solitary monument perhaps the Washington monument? Came into view….the object, an obelisk?…expanded exponentially, ballooned out into a large rectangular shape….it slowly rose …rapidly replacing the 2D image with a virtual 3D photo which quickly created an intricate set of linear, horizontal, and vertical lines enveloping the massive marvel…with a prominent point in the center of the roofline.... She wanted to scream as the surreal rendering registered in her over active imagination...the fatal flight seemed to be nearing an abrupt end....the airliner destined to take out the entire hotel atop the massive mound.... It must be a dream! It must be she reasoned....as she was slowly sucked inside the structure...like a spirit....or wispy cloud.....she tried to close her eyes...expecting the inevitable; to be splattered all over the ornate architectural moldings....a macabre bloody mess dripping from the eavestrough.... onto the fresh white fallen snow....there seemed no way out of the nightmare....a never ending circle ...no matter how far she roamed...she always returned to the wretched symbol... It tapped her sanity, her very essence.....the uncontrollable black hole drew her into it's interior...she passed through the permeable membrane without a scratch or scar. Perhaps she'd been flung into an open window? Why had she survived?...and where were all the other passengers? Perished in the fiery inferno? But she saw no crash site nearby; dripping in sweat she wanted to scream.... Her weak weary vocal chords would not permit it...Speechless, she stared into space, her eyes wide shut…She felt something tugging on her head…perhaps the overhead oxygen masks….her eyes suddenly opened. She found herself in the same dark decrepit predicament she was in prior to her departure and dreamy flight. She tried to remove the persistent tugging in her tussled disheveled head of hair. Bats, in the belfry? Was she going mad? She saw the dark silhouette in front of her… a grizzly bear?…about to drag her to her death… from her sleeping bag? Or from the hotel? how could an animal have gotten into ….she reached for the axe but it was not there…she patted the wet damp hardwood floor…covered in her sweat or blood? Before she realized what was upon her… the powerful predator began to drag her off down the hall…She fought feverishly, kicking, fighting in a frenzy; her feet found no resistance as she slid along the slippery floor on her rump…ripping the delicate fabric of her evening gown…from the rug burns……..it then donned on her, that her husband had found her…defenseless, frightened…running a fever? A hand full of hair in one hand, wielding the razor sharp axe in the other, the crazed caveman

dragged his prey off toward the enclosure.
Room 321....the final countdown...she desperately
sought to free herself from his relentless greedy
grip. She tried to spread her wings and fly...or
spread her legs as an expandable impediment to
prevent her entry into the chamber. He kicked the
door open...with one quick swift swoop, like a
determined kicker to insure the winning convert in
the Super Bowl? He'd never convince her to
convert to his crazy cult like customs....he dropped
his axe, then grabbed her hair with his free hand
and flung her with superhuman strength onto the
bed.. She hit the bedpost hard...out like a light.
This left him to prepare her bath. The bubbling
boiling oil was still hot...but he preferred to
surprise her and really light her fire! He grabbed
the axe and shattered one of the chairs from their
former tryst at the table for two by the window and
hacked it into large slivers. He tore the kindling
apart and got down on his knees to place it on the
splattered tiled ensuite floor around the deep basin.
He fumbled in his pockets for a lighter...but found
nothing, he wasn't a smoker...he realized. In lieu
of a lighter, the light bulb dimly went on above his

head. Of course! He sought a pack of matches…the POW must provide one in each ashtray! He rose to his feet, bent down to pick up the axe..and nearly passed out from the sudden rush of blood to his head. As he turned around to enter the bedroom chamber…

"Rock seee?" The runaway bride had bolted from the chamber of horrors and taken the bed sheets with her resourcefully. Escape from an upper story? she'd freeze to death in her flimsy fall fashions he felt. He turned to the ensuite. Pity, he thought to himself…the perfect ending to a particularly taxing ordeal. A done deal he thought to himself…fate may have dealt him a bad hand. Yet, realized the native tarot cards were rather accurate in the depiction of the carnage and mayhem that ensued. The utter and complete chaos that he found himself in the midst of, made him much more appreciative of the medicine man. By the way, where was he now? Why was he always absent in the midst of a crisis? Avoiding a confrontation? Or well aware of the tangled web each couple wove that entered the hallowed haunted halls. He always knew when to enter the premises, after the fact. In fact, perhaps he was the part taker to the perilous plots? Waiting for the perfect moment to intervene…then vanish with his new bride, Pocahontas, slung over his shoulders? He seemed to anticipate every angle of the clash of the couple, the growing anxiety and dramatic acts. They had seemingly survived the first and second acts nearly tearing out each other's throats in lieu of a captive audience. Yet where and when the final curtain call would take place he knew not. He wiped the blood, sweat and tears from his brow, and brushed the debris from his hands. Her strong scent still lingered all over him and seemed to penetrate the very pores of the palace. He stopped to catch his breath…certain she'd given up…He left the Lakeview Suite dejected yet determined to deliver his damsel in distress. His curious courtly gestures…and precoital practices left a lot to be desired, yet he was in no shape or mental state to distinguish the difference as he slowly crept down the hallway to begin the pursuit of his prey anew. With renewed strength from the brief interlude, he noticed several open doorways… An icy chilly draft delivered a rude awakening to the cunning clinician…like a solid slap on the cheeks. The frosty breeze frisked and clawed on his face..as if to signify what he'd missed if the misses had made her intentions clear to him. In her defenseless state, she had put up little resistance and rather ran from the fray in her frail condition. She was hardly in a position for a prolonged challenge he thought. He entered the next room and discovered an open window. He leaned out grateful she hadn't fallen from the third floor, likely fatal on the slippery slope or impaling herself on a sharp projection near the parking lot below. Glad there was no evidence of egress, not a shred of a bed sheet.. he slammed the sash…the window frozen shut…He left the room empty handed to resume his search. The next guest room door stood ajar…quite the clever opponent, he applauded the methods to her madness.. mixing him up, presumably confusing him, stalling him, buying precious time. He bashed the door like an irate bear breaking into a cabin's kitchen, desperately foraging for berries before slipping into hibernation. Once again his cunning concubine had given him the slip…in a deadly game of deception, desperate to get out alive or at least return to a stale mate? He continued the chase, the musical doors, like musical chairs made more sense. He focused his attention for the first time and recalled the room numbers like a faithful servant of the POW.. making his rounds for the evening…But, rather than a polite rapping at a respected guest's door, he brought the brunt of his weight in the forceful entry into each chamber. Once again, the vacant, frosty ice box…brought him little relief. His elusive enchantress was nowhere to be found.. not a stitch of slinky, black seductive clothing…as per their previous playful antics, nor a white strip of shredded bed sheets…he needed a sign, a signal, something to assure him she was still leading him on in her provocative albeit perilous teasing tactics. He continued to peruse the premises ….one room at a time…he'd be up all night if that's what it took to reclaim her trust or at least capture her attention. Where was she he wondered? He continued his relentless quest to come up with even a stitch of evidence she was ever here…Unlike the lingering virtual visions, apparitions prancing about….practicing their peculiar pesky pranks to p…off a guest. The ghosts had the run of the mansion, anything but your run of the mill motel or run down road side rooms. The regal residence slowly shed it's skin as he penetrated each chamber. Yet the dirty little sordid secrets contained within each room remained nothing more than rumors or old wives' tales. He desperately hoped he'd find her before she'd become one.

7: Chiller

"It reminded me of his Uncle Seamus,
the notorious and poetic drunk, who
would sit down at the breakfast table
the morning after a bender, drain a
bottle of stout and say, 'Ah the chill
of consciousness returns'."
- Molly O'Neill

Roxy had reached her wit's end...and came full
circle through the chamber of horrors, back to
square one. She stood in the midst of the mess hall.
The bleeding model of he POW, first and foremost
on her mind, bothered her. She had to get out,
make a break for it. The precious seconds she had

won by bamboozling her bearish blood thirsty bozo, whittled away. The sands of time slowly dropped in the horrific hourglass, like the pit and the pendulum…ticking.. slowly slicing at her mid section…She felt a gut wrenching pain sick to the pit of her stomach…faced with the inevitable end.. She peered onto the desolate deathly chilly landscape outside. The POW lights extended to the perimeter of the mesa, the cliffs, beyond, likely a deadly drop off to the water's edge. Across the endless plain barren wasteland of Enchanted Bay, she spotted something…a subtle twinkling. Odd, a porch light? Perhaps the Killroy Innkeeper had returned or remained, having second thoughts about their resilience, a safety net for the honeymooners. RD had mentioned the lodge usually stayed open year round. That must be it. Or perhaps the undertaker had stayed, given the heads up of the horrific ordeal, albeit business for him. She blotted the gruesome thought from her mind. She decided to make a break for it…across the narrow gap separating her from the hellish nightmare and the sleepy town of Wutherington nestled in the hollow glacial basin. She had no time or intention to go grab her coat from the chamber of horrors inhabited by her ghastly significant other. All she had on were the tattered rags on her back, the dress ripped down to the great divide between the arch of her butt cheeks and a handful of bed sheets. She opted for the other side of the bay. The equation seemed to make sense, escape = life…remain meant certain death. She made a fateful break and bolted for the back exit. The door seemed frozen shut…resourcefully she'd extracted the axe before her husband had an opportunity to hone his chopping skills. Chop chop she told her self still tormented by disgusting thoughts of death and dismemberment. She'd be one member to avoid the wretched indoctrination into his private hellish club. She raised her weary arms yet found the strength to drive the razor sharp blade deep into the aging door. Resolutely she continued to chip away at the wooden planks like the last leftovers of the vessel that became trapped in the ice floes. The HMS resolute…returned home…and as a token of appreciation, hewn into the precious desk that graced the Oval office with it's presence… With renewed strength she severed

the large barrier. The icy frosty breeze frisked
at her exposed flesh like an intruder trying to gain
entry or perhaps the police arriving in the nick of
time to disarm the perpetrator of the crime. If only;
she wished she were anywhere but here…as if in
unison, she cracked the door…as did her husband
still lost in the upper rafters around the lobby…
yanking the door knobs, breaking and entering at
will…rummaging through the desolate icy rooms..
in a futile attempt to find her. She found the
door finally fell apart, splitting in two. She
chuckled…just like her husband. .when and how
the split occurred did not dawn on her as she
crept through the narrow aperture. The bitter cold
brought her to a fully frightened state. She knew it
was now or never…a race against the clock to
survive. Every second counted…drawing her
nearer to an inevitable surreal state of suspended
animation, cryogenically preserved ironically not
far from the Crypt Lake landing trail head she
chuckled. A chip off the block she laughed, a
cavewoman they'd have to extract with an ice pick,
presumably the one from the very Weeping
Willow. She was surprised to retain any semblance

of sanity or sense of humor in the midst of the hellish nightmare. Perhaps there was still hope? Something she clung onto as she neared the precipice. The steep sharp drop off brought her to the edge of reason. Peering out over the panoramic point, she perused the landscape for a way down. There was no easy way out of this precarious predicament she feared. Her chances kept slipping away with every icy breath she took. To compound the problem, the bitter cold consumed her. She couldn't stand it…then hurried back to the hotel… The blood red hue that oozed from the large lobby window panes hung over the hillside like a forlorn passenger of a red eye flight. Hung over from a heavy heart? She had very little time. A thought occurred to her.. why not go with the flow…why go against the grain? What she needed was a toboggan, to sail down the slippery dangerous slope. The momentum might send me clear across to the dock on the other side of the bay. The tide and her luck was turning she felt. Good tidings, a blessing in disguise? She dispelled any doubt she had and beelined for the back entrance. Cautiously she crawled through the entrance etched out of the wood, careful not to arouse the angry beast within. Her eyes darted around the kitchen, cluttered with pots, pans, shards of shattered porcelain plates. The cookie sheets. A harbinger of hope rather than the wretched reminders of her macabre masterpiece? She raced to the counter. Some of the large aluminum sheets were still warm to the touch. She preferred the untouched room temperature surfaces...not sure if the hot plates would serve her purpose. She looked at the large rectangular metal sections long and hard, like Amelia Earhardt, as if pondering traversing the Pacific in a makeshift manmade flying jalopy. Just what the doctor ordered she concurred. The sheets would serve her purpose perfectly she predicted. She ripped several strands of bed sheets and lay them under the width of each sheet as if gift wrapping a present. The peculiar present may not delight any child in the townsite, on Christmas morn, but it delighted her immensely. She moved the large aerodynamic surfboard like surfaces outside. To test her theory, she placed both feet on top of the center of gravity of each surface, she had calculated. Balancing with her legs spread eagle she prepared to test her hypothesis. She approached the edge of the cliff, inspecting the slope. Across the bay, the bright light like the Star over Bethlehem or comparable beacon denoting the nativity scene would suffice. She then reached down to wrap her feet in swaddling. She teetered over the precipice, about to send herself gift wrapped special delivery to the town folk. She hoped she'd have enough momentum to sail half way across the bay using the boathouse as a landmark like a marker buoy. She lined up her target…and took a deep breath.

The burly beast became obnoxiously boisterous. He hadn't bothered to knock on any of the last doors at the end of the hall and gave up. She had given him the slip.. and slipped back into the kitchen obviously. Why it had taken so long to come up with this brilliant revelation disturbed him. He hustled down the stairs…startled by the icy breeze coming from the roastiest toastiest room in the entire retreat. He gazed at the gaping hole formed in the back exit and presumed a predator, namely one ornery old black or grizzly bear had gained entry. He peered around the room

apprehensively…awaiting come what may
from a corner, or crevice in the kitchen. The
sudden twist in fate unnerved him. The hunter now
the hunted? The hotel left nothing to chance. It
seemed to cover it's tracks to eradicate it's
residents and remove any remnant of their visits.
The gruesome prospect of being dragged off into a
dark den as leftovers lingered foremost on his
mind…The soused sleuth sensed that it may have
already claimed it's first victim…as he noticed the
long linear lines leading from the back door.
A large mass, perhaps the predator; had poked
about in the fridge and maneuvered an entire side
of fresh venison, presumably as large as a buffalo
or bison he estimated from the size of the swath in
the snow. In the distance he noticed an object
waving it's arms…the helpless prey about to take
the plunge, pulled over the cliff, in a fateful leap of
faith. His bloodshot bleary eyes scoped the galley
of any sign of his gal. It didn't sink into his
confused cluttered cranium for a few seconds, that
the feisty female…overgrown goose, or mallard
may in fact be his wife. The runaway bride teetered
at the end of the runway with only one light to

guide her home.

"What's a duck doing out there?" he declared, disoriented, distraught. He needed another drink, to replenish his radiator. The antifreeze he had in mind would neither warm his innards nor save him from the buzzards as Harley Brown oft stated.

"May the joy juice in your gizzard
keep you warm in a blizzard…
and the vultures and buzzards
never gitcha….."''.

Yet the damn delusions drove him to drown his sorrows. He strode shakily toward the Weeping Willow lounge, one eye on the poor creature hovering over the ledge in obvious pain. It was furiously waving it's arms in a futile attempt to flee…or fly? An emu or ostrich stood no chance of survival in the harsh frigid frozen wasteland he figured. But it might serve his purpose well. He'd pluck every feather from the feisty overgrown pheasant and surprise his wife at dinner. In lieu of a turkey, he'd serve a winged Wutherington what ever with all the trimmings…then fell flat on his face. He had to hurry before it got away. He rushed out the back exit to brave the ghastly cold elements in pursuit of his prey. He found the going rough…as he repeatedly sank to his knees. How the bird ever got as far as it did was a complete mystery to him…as he snuck up on the fine feathered pheasant.

"It's now or never….Jeronimooooooo!" ejaculated his excited feathery fray suddenly. It didn't don on him until he'd reached the edge of the precipice and flung his arms around, the figment of his imagination; that he realized his wife had given him the slip again, literally. The two top heavy toboggans, slid neck and neck in a tie, a stalemate…whooshing down the wuthering windy heights with a vengeance. The winner impossible to determine. It was a dead heat…or rather icy indecisive state of confusion. It did not deter him from giving chase. He'd never let his wife get away again he swore on his…grave? He caught a glimpse of a porch light he presumed either Jebb, the undertaker who took much pride in his work, perhaps preparing a special parting gift…for a loved one? He'd be the only one up at this ungodly hour he surmised.

He knew he had to get her back inside in a

hurry or they'd both be preserved in the permafrost …..forever ..he already halfway there in his present pickled state. He feared falling and not ever getting up, drifting off into a deathly slumber.. as he maneuvered over the larger rocks at the base of the cliff. How she'd escaped a calamity was beyond his intoxicated intuition to comprehend. He'd heard of sea otters ramming the rocks like wild animals butting heads fighting fiercely for a mate. Taking a fatal plunge, a pontoon may shear from the undercarriage of an aircraft attempting a precarious two point landing at the lake's end. The other side of the border proved even less passable. If not by air, by foot or beast of burden proved practically impossible. A chance encounter with the ursus horribilis, coming across the path of the gruesome giant grizzly bear, the chances dropped from slim to nil. In fact, one would have a better chance dropping dead…or presumed perfect immobility in a deadly game of truth or dare.

"I have just the thing waiting to warm your bones" as he watched the silver bullets beeline and blaze a trail over the sparkling snow across the bay. The full moon glowed brightly overhead and

allowed any eyewitness snippets of the surreal
scene. It also cast an eerie radiance on the
respected wretched haunted hotel. It had already
slipped into considerable disrepair and ruin during
the short duration of their stay. The massive red
bloodshot panes, like large luminous lanterns
illuminated the surrounding hilltop in an eerie red
hue. It's mesmerizing hypnotizing stare from atop
the mesa made him uneasy as he made his way
sluggishly through the snow. Each step took it's
toll tapping his energy..as he stepped to the water's
edge he wondered if he'd get his feet wet. How
thick in fact was the cover of ice on the deceptively
feathery light frosted coating? He tread on thin ice
he feared, his relationship surely in ruin, on the
rocks! He was resolved, determined to rescue her
if not from himself, then a tragic dunking.. in the
liquid deep freeze! He desperately danced over the
deceptively slippery white surface. A slippery
underlying sheen made the passage particularly
perilous and impeding his progress as he seemed to
slide one step back for each foot thrust forward.
Roxy had made real progress as the momentum of
her sled propelled her almost halfway across the

wide track like a legendary Olympic luge or downhill slalom competitor.

"Come on, come on" she encouraged the silver bullets. The icy breeze deprived her of oxygen as she gasped, concealing her face in the white sheets that she'd resourcefully wrapped around her. She looked like an enchanting Egyptian mummy or a giant 'ice worm' poking it's head from the frosty icy depths scouring the surface for it's next victim. The antics of the animal caught the attention of an unruly restless resident rummaging through the boathouse. Dressed in a heavy parka, native moccasins, hand made leather skin gloves. His snowshoes leaned against the tool shed door. Running Deer had gone to get some desperately needed tools to fix a few things around the hotel. The hotel staff had left him very few implements to address the needs of the regal residence in lieu of the well heeled guests' fondue forks or countless salad forks and elegant dinner ware to gobble up the pricey Beluga caviar and tasty expensive truffle. Or jewelers tools to tune the fine treasure trove of accessories they'd hauled to the hotel. There was a complete lack of even the smallest

screwdriver in the 9 month off season amongst
the packed boxes in anticipation of the next season.

His eyes caught a glimpse of the humungous
white animal hardly hopping across the frozen
lake. A giant white rabbit? Definitely a bad omen
he knew; a harbinger of death. He couldn't believe
his eyes, rubbed them gently for a few seconds. He
hadn't indulged in any fire water he'd saved
especially for these special occasions when the
guests kept him up all night. He thought nothing of
the notorious nemesis as it slipped from view..just
a figment of his imagination he reasoned and went
back about his business. He dug a little deeper in
the collection of naval nostalgia, and came up with
an old steering wheel.. presumably from the Miss
Wutherington. He reassessed the age of the small
steering mechanism tightly wound with a
continuous strand of rope. A few frayed edges..
formed a perfect 'cross' or four spoked support
lattice work in the center of the small circle.

"St Mary's Coxcomb."

He held it firmly and figured it was much older,
conceivably from the original wreck of the
Germaine which was laid to rest following a

thriving treacherous trek across the US-CDN border during the prohibition c 1920's, running rum and other alcoholic beverages to the locals and some of the crews in the old lumber mills to while away the long bitter cold nights. Long since sunk, scuttled somewhere in the middle of Enchanted Bay, the bow in some 60' of water, the stern sat ass end up in some 20', he couldn't recall which end was which? Technically an easy dive, if you knew where to look. He'd never bothered, preferring the simple pleasures of life, above board. Anything he could touch, see and smell. The basic creature comforts he could cram into a teepee next to a stream of cool clear running water. All the accessories, rotting furniture riddled with termites, the headboards, the pleasures of the idle rich he considered superfluous, merely useless adornments that made no sense whatsoever.

Roxy, on the other hand had enjoyed a life in the lap of luxury. This was her first real challenge that now proved to be a life threatening test. Her trek had only taken her about halfway to her intended target. Fortunately she'd come this far and not made the 'breakthrough' she feared and dreaded,

going where only eagles dare, she slowly
lowered herself onto the large shiny surfaces like
an agile surfer. With pronounced arm motions..like
Michael Phelps, she ploughed her way across the
slippery surface like a feisty furry seal toward an
imaginary finish line somewhere near a bright
shining porch light. Luckily someone had left it on
to guide her home. She could hardly wait to get out
of this unsightly albeit well worn woven life
preserver. The multi layered wrappings likely
saved her from certain death as she laboriously
inched her way to the water's edge with each
breast stroke. Her extremities however were
getting weary and numb. She knew not how much
longer she could hold out. Her partner in crime in
hot pursuit also felt the frosty fickle fingers of fate
tighten their grip around him. It felt as if hell had
frozen over. The miserable menacing bitter breeze
that blew down the steep mountainsides into the
town of Wutherington had always swept an unwary
cross country skier to their deaths. The deceptively
long distances and harsh inclemental weather
conditions continually claimed it's victims. From
the onset of the surprisingly early onset of snow

this season, even a careless trapper could succumb to the harsh clime if caught unawares.

Impossible to continue, he made the decision to turn back…grab a few silver bullets and follow her lead. It was ludicrous he realized, to attempt to cover the treacherous albeit flat terrain, on foot. The fear of falling through the ice like the fateful plunge of a fearless snowmobiler convinced him. His chance of waddling his way across the waterway like his mate made sense. What was good for the goose was good for the gander. Or visa versa… if only to ward off any pesky were-wolves that still lurked about. Their blood curdling howls could be heard for miles as they echoed and careened through the carved canyons. He hustled about but lost his footing. He had fallen and couldn't get up….he feared even a team of rescuers would trample over his remains. He'd likely be found by a band of ravenous dogs…Determined not to become bone meal or wild dog treats, he gathered what little strength he could summon and slowly rose form the slippery teflon like coated terrain. Like a curious chipmunk scouring the lay of the land for a tasty treat, he peered at his pride and joy, just a few hundred yards ahead of him...near where he recalled the rum runner had run out of luck. Lady luck seemed to be on her side as she continued to take long slow steady strides traversing the surface like a confident curler at a coveted bonspiel or a hefty Hawaiian canoeist in his outrigger. In lieu of the small side car, or side saddle, the extra slippery sheet assisted her over a hump. Her thoughts turned to a warm Tahitian or Polynesian beach...to take her mind off the incessant icy winds that nipped at her bony digits...her fingernails broken off, her fingertips now bleeding from clawing her way across hell's frozen wasteland. She was caught between a rock and a hard place...in the middle of the bay. Enchanting was hardly the word she'd use for the enlightening near death experience. Midway from any shoreline...a lingering thought crept into her mind, it followed her like the ever present funeral director...whose porch light appeared as the only harbinger of hope now. She'd totally lost her bearings and dared not look back in anger over her shoulder at the root of all her problems in the first place. The regal wretched residence..that kept a close watch over Wutherington's town folk…with an ever present, penetrating glare… Perhaps there was no escape? Once one entered into no man's land, the tiny protected spit of land butting against the bold rugged Rockies at 'land's end', the final countdown had already commenced. Get in and out quickly while you still can. This had been anything but a short and sweet stay. Come to think of it, she had no idea how long she'd been out here…Her sense of time slowly vanished as a soothing warmth enveloped her…She knew she had to keep moving, or she'd succumb to the sinister deep sleep, and certain death. Which fate the worse of two evils? Perhaps he'd claim the coveted prize either way. No matter, if she'd stayed to be skewered alive by the butcher or fall asleep in sweet slumber. It seemed the least painful of the two options rather than stay awake partially anaesthetized at the hands of the sloppy surgeon slobbering and drooling all over her like some rabid dog, she preferred her remedy. The painless prescription should she fail to reach the finish line would soon end her misery. She wondered what might have been clawing her way with every ounce of her strength that remained before he'd lose consciousness…and felt somewhat satisfied. She, like her husband, had reached every goal she'd set out to achieve. She felt saddened she'd never experience the labor pains of childbirth albeit could clearly imagine the horrific pain…if this nightmare was any indicator, a litmus or pregnancy test, leading to the day of deliverance. Nor would she be around to see her children grow up. She'd wanted at least two rug rats to tend and take care of, take them on long strolls in their cute naval outfits or Halloween costumes. Nurture them through the long formative years of their youth. To provide a warm loving nurturing environment encouraging their every whim and wish…She wished she'd stayed at home. He could have penned his nightmarish novel completely on his own, in solitary confinement.. let him be…purge the powerful demons that lurked in the deep dark recesses of his mind. Mind you, his lectures usually put her to sleep. She dreaded the words, now her worst enemy and tried to turn her thoughts to more pleasant memories. The first intimate moments when she knew they were meant for each other.

Divine intervention? Hardly, the horned beast, the devil certainly deserved all the credit for disrupting their meticulously mapped out carefree prescription to get away from it all. Maybe there was no true escape. We were all just prisoners of our devices, and unsavory sinister vices. The POW had simply found a way to unleash the demons. Satisfying it's and it's inhabitants most sinister thoughts and cravings. She had to stay awake. whatever it took….. keep talking to yourself Roxy rock on…her pace quickened considerably form her little pep talk. Right on.. her energy dissipated …her pace slowed as she sensed her own finiteness.. his inspiration? Perhaps only for his penmanship, his wretched writings, the writing was on the walls of the hotel… she felt…. In their ship of fools. He fooled no one…not even the cards. They'd come up in the same suit, the same sinister variation she felt. Their fate had been determined many moons ago…she should have seen it coming all along. The talented apothecary apache's enlightenment angered her. Why she hadn't had the foresight to see through his petty ploys. She saw right through her husband …like all the other ghosts and goblins that resided in the regal residence, appearances and apparitions were deceiving. Perhaps a little scary at first, but in time she'd learned to uncover his deep dark secrets, as he did hers. One mustn't judge a book by it's cover he harped on continually. His cleverly crafted twist and turns, taking the audience on a mind numbing, mind bending roller coaster ride. This was just another one in a long line of special effects intended to dazzle her. All the fancy gala dinners and escapes he'd planned for her…in his lengthy itineraries that unraveled like the Dead Sea Scrolls meant nothing now. She'd soon meet her maker.. permanently preserved in the permafrost like a museum oddity. Her true value not realized for another thousand years. Odd, she'd never even been to a museum with the buffoon,

> "There once was a brainy baboon,
>
> who always breathed down a bassoon,
>
> for he said it appears,
>
> that in billions of years,
>
> I shall certainly hit on a tune."

Ezra Pound, as she continued to pound her clenched fist down on the ice defiantly. She'd not surrendered her last and final breath yet …albeit even the bright full moon beams brought her little relief. The previous shimmering sheen and kaleidoscope of color that glittered on the surface lost it's luster. Her enthusiasm and zest for life waned like the ebb and flow of the tide. The tide was irreversibly turning in favor of the grim reaper she felt…as he sought his next victim. If the demented dentist's delightful dinner party did not poison and put to rest any part takers, she knew that by the end of the evening her ordeal would. Would she live to tell her tall tales to her kids, or grand kids? she wondered. The hotel could have him. Her husband, lock stock and barrel of rum, yo ho , ho…

"Good riddance…" she yelled irritably.

"Mustn't fall asleep" she softly muttered to herself about to drift off into the sweet netherlands of her subconscious. She arranged the rest of her wrappings…into a tight roll underneath her head like a pillow. Sleeping beauty wouldn't want to be disturbed for the next.. oh say, thousand years or so…Don't bother to set the alarm…the damn clock, nor any form of radio reception didn't reach the remote spot anyway. A million thoughts went through her mind…The countless guests, ghosts, ghouls and goblins could raise a toast to her… "drink to me, drink to my health you know I can't drink any more.."

It sounded like something her husband would or had said….somewhere along the long and winding road to Wutherington. The end was near she felt…. RD spotted the faint outline of the comical clown still in pursuit of his mistress. Like a maniacal Mexican jumping bean, he continued to hop along…or maybe it was an ice worm indeed? He'd never seen one that wasn't well camouflaged. Why he could pick this one off…if only he had his trusty bow and arrow.

"Oh those honeymooners!" he announced, then laughed out loud. The disoriented dentist..did not take his eyes off his wife. Her powerful breast strokes had ceased.. He had to hurry to reach her, for he knew she'd soon succumb to the bitter icy breeze that blew through the valley like a luxurious intoxicating alcoholic cloud…setting everything at ease in a sea of tranquility… Roxy had a strange feeling, another aura?

clairsentience, or clairvoyance. She strained to listen to the sounds of silence. She could only hear her heart thumping inside her chest…yet it soon became crystal clear that the ice was cracking all around her.

"There she goes" declared as he saw Roxy swallowed up and disappear through the ice.

"Rockseee, don't leave meeeee" echoed down through the entire valley..

8: Diving

> I think you have to know who you are.
> Get to know the monster that lives in
> your soul, dive deep into your soul and
> explore it."
> - Tori Amos

The dentist stood in disbelief for but a second before he raced toward the sharp edges of the ice and her last known position.

Roxy's body was given the shock and jolt of it's life, like receiving a misaligned jump start; the electricity surged through her lifeless frame. She had to act fast unfurling the soaked white bed sheets sinking rapidly like a stone into the deathly cold depths. She was amazed she hadn't had a heart attack instantly from the defibrillating action of the icy fluid circulating all around her chest.

"My own brain to me is the most unaccountable of machinery –always buzzing, humming, soaring, roaring, diving, and then buried in mud. And why? What's this passion for?" (Virginia Woolf) The prospect of death by choking rather than chocolate left her craving every last breath….as she tied the loose ends of the sheets in a knot. This was not the escape route she envisioned…in fact her eyes stung…and saw only the white ripped chord, her life line, close to her…as she descended. She'd succumb to a series of stupid choices she made… as she nodded off….Unable to provoke her body to respond…she soon realized they'd likely never find her in the frozen fluid...and hit rock bottom …in actuality lodged either half of her drenched torso over a rusty rotting handrail…almost a century old. The weight of the water crushing her, squeezing every ounce of strength from her body sent her into a tail spin. Roxy slowly lost consciousness in the dark depths coming to the complete acceptance that this was indeed the end.

RD, momentarily stunned, watched the events unfold in slow motion, sprung into action. He rummaged through the rigging, and tackle to see what he'd come up with. Every second counted. He found rope, yards, miles of it. Testing the strength he pulled either end taut...as if to test the strength of it for a final series of knots of a heavy hangman's noose. Neither end ceded as he tugged the sturdy rope he'd used countless times to lasso the dock and tie each vessel to the dock. Why' it could easily suspend a baby grand piano in mid air! He fumbled unfurling a mile of the tightly wound rope like and Indian rope charmer. In lieu of his magic flute, only his trusty stainless steel blade bearing an ornately carved buffalo bison bone handle may yet determine her fate. The buffalo symbolized the very essence of his way of life. The key figure in the sun dance, the very sustenance, the meat, the skins for tepees, the fur for their warm parkas and clothes...and essentially all the materials for tools for their daily survival. It certainly came in handy now. It's power to cure soon put to the test.

Dr Gum reached the fatal landmark…where she had fallen through the ice. He peered down into the dark abyss. There was no sign of her other than the white bed sheet, her lifeline, the golden chord if her could get to her in time. She'd been under for several minutes, likely already drowned. He turned and looked about…but caught only the glimpse of the hideous hotel…aglow in the ghastly red hue …as if fueled, enflamed by one final act the couple was compelled to fulfill during their very short stay. The guests hadn't been in the hotel for more than a month, driven to their deaths by the demonic presence, perpetually perpetrating the perilous pranks in the palatial prison. He looked back in anger defiantly, then took a swig from a bottle of whiskey he'd stuffed in his coat pocket to keep him warm. One last big gulp of air followed by the bitter medicine. This was the end, his only friend now, RD was nowhere to be found. In hindsight, he'd likely stayed at the Killroy Lodge, yet knew deep down in the back of his mind, there was no safe haven in Wutherington, away from the leering crazed presence of the palace on Prominence

Way.......He tossed the bottle into the snow
then removed his formal dinner jacket in one final
foolhardy act. Then took the leap of faith as he
stepped out as if from the stern of a vessel during a
routine diving expedition. Into the icy darkness,
he'd soon join his wife in the abyss approaching
absolute zero. He felt the fingers of death grab him
and swallow him alive ...whole ....he dipped down
head first in a futile attempt to find her...by
following the taut life line that disappeared into the
murky dark depths...

RD had crept up on him holding the ends of the
unraveled rope...in one final sneak attack to put
him out of his misery?

"Wait, you fool!"

The words reverberated both over and under the
ice...like a wretched macabre message...a decree
to announce the answer...and fulfillment of the
Blackfoot prophecy.

The hardy fool used the scant sliver of light to
grope and feel his way along the white life line
dropping like a stone. He'd hit rock bottom soon if
it weren't for his resourceful reach out into the
dark...He found a rail wrapped around the ship

presumably the promenade deck at the stern of the vessel some 20' below the surface. What were the odds? His chances of ever finding his wife in the fateful few seconds that remained ere he lost consciousness were far and few between. He'd soon forever rest next to her in peace at the bottom of Enchanted Bay. "In diving to the bottom of pleasure we bring up more gravel than pearls." (Honore de Balzac)

The seasoned visionary practiced in the art of survival, the medicine man for all seasons, held St Mary's Coxcomb in front of him, he dropped to his knees. In a final futile gesture….near the sight of the dynamic duo's disappearance, he affixed the frayed ends of the rope tightly around the center of the steering wheel. He wrapped them around it and tied a knot…praying it would hold…then inched toward the edge of the ice on all fours as if preying upon a small camouflaged rodent. He blotted the white rabbit from his mind. RD would not let the harbinger of doom claim another victim, besides the card did not appear at the séance. He placed his chances at slim to nil and prayed as he lowered the noose. The moonlight on the water, the oracle had already spoken he assumed as he glanced back up to the silent sentinel…The large reddish luminous orbs seems to observe his every move, never once letting him out of it's sight…..

"Here goes nothing!" as he peered past the hotel at the spirit in the sky. Hopefully the Buffalo would grant him this one wish…he didn't want it to end this way; fishing a few frozen corpses from the depths of the any thing but enchanting bay. Dr Gum was at the end of his rope….a few last breaths…free falling, an unbelievable feeling, drowning…unencumbered, free from the restraints of the world. He felt like letting go…as he drifted off, down…down…rigor mortis would soon set in. He bumped into a soft mass; he reached down and groped the soft fold, he'd grabbed his wife's round ass. He hung onto her waist as if to mount her in a mad necrophiliac motion, intent to never let her go….

Roxy had slipped into a state of suspended animation, accepting the fact…slowly allowing the cryopreservative fluid to fill her lungs….she choked briefly…yet found the feeling quite pleasant.. as her mind diverted her attention and attenuated all the pain and suffering she'd experienced throughout her short lifespan. She roamed the hills and valleys free as a bird, soaring like an eagle, the chief of all the creatures of the air, the guardian of the people over all evil. Her gossamer wings raised her as if weightless above the clouds...and off into the ether...nearer the eternal omnipotent presence... She accepted whatever fate came her way. The nirvana like interlude abruptly abated as she felt the weight of the world not only upon her shoulders, but her butt. Her spirit was suddenly crushed...as the liquid was forced out and expelled from her lungs... was an emergency medical team trying to revive her she wondered? Pounding her chest in one desperate attempt to bring her back to life? She refused to comply..opting for the latter choice...consenting to be taken into the hereafter. She did not fight the feeling...

Her husband hung onto her in a 'warm' embrace, bracing himself...to avoid a 'fatal' fall? To the frozen rocky bottom. He'd sunk so low....and felt responsible for driving them both over the edge ...to their deaths....yet his feelings of doubt, guilt

and despair soon subsided. The tragedy erased
like a tabula rasa, a clean slate… as his thoughts
turned to his earliest cherished childhood and
earlier memories of birth…The birth pangs his
wife may never know…as he popped out of the
warm wet womb like a small slippery porpoise.
The purpose of his life unknown least of all to
himself. He may have found it during his early
formative years, as a youngster playing the part of
aspiring doctor, some of the neighborhood kids the
patients…The precocious youth played the role
well, assuming the charismatic part of the
character. His early teens took him on numerous
global treks with his parents. Hiking through
nature, ascending to the tips of the very mountains
that now looked down upon him like disgruntled
gods. The very lake on which he'd honed his chair
side skills, his bedside manner, helping the
countless passengers onboard, to safely bring them
to the other side to Crypt landing. Now dunked in
the very spot he'd always referred to during his
commentary on the two hour tour. Such a fateful
trip from the tiny port. His actions were so out of
character…why in the world had he been so brash

and brazen, bringing his bride here? To this haunted unnatural man made mausoleum. The perfect honeymoon hideaway where the dear and the antelope played…he had to bring his beloved bride to the place where he grew up. Where the rabble rouser ran wild and free…unfettered by the chains and restraints of the world, everything the hotel represented. The imposed man made time constraints and restrictions. "Publishers are demons, there's no doubt about it." (William Jamse, American philosopher) as he perused the pages of his most recent past. Compelled to crank out the chilling tale…in a couple months drove him to drink heavily, indulge in the delicious taunting intoxicating elixir. Slowly eroding, etching away all rhyme or reason for his reason d'etre as he eked out an existence….giving up all that he had. His former trophies such as his wife, like all the other awards and achievements were now just flotsam and jetsom tossed overboard amongst all the other baggage at the bottom of the bay. He leafed through the pages, the previous memories he'd compiled, returning to earlier, the most recent recollections. The gradual transition from a thriving, successful practice to a shoddy, solitary one man show, confined to completing a few patient charts. His was so consumed by his overactive imagination…he felt he had to get away from it all, the call of the wild? Or something much more chilling, sinister? The hotel compelled him to come and pen the final crazy chapter of his life… in a furious frenzy, bamboozled by the booze, inebriated by wanton desires of his wife…. Why? had he come full circle?…to complete some demonic preordained plan? As he turned over a new leaf in his mind, he balanced on her back, in a macabre back massage, managing to glance back up. The small dimly lit aperture seemed like an unattainable goal, miles above, an unreachable eternity away. Realizing the imminent end of the manuscript…was writing itself, he relished in the few fond memories in the few brief moments that remained.

"I've got one shot" said Running Deer shivering in his boots…his fingers nearly frozen stiff as he secured the line then leaned cautiously over the edge. The dead weight sunk down…down..down… he reckoned he'd hit their dead bodies in a couple seconds…

The dreary disoriented dentist took one last look up into the small tunnel of light…as if to accept the fact…relinquishing his life…to his maker… and saw a strange albeit reassuring sight…a 'cross' slowly came into view. He even imagined he saw the face of JC, the center of the apparition. His anxiety ceased accepting the fact of his and her finiteness. St Mary's Coxcomb, knocked him on the noggin. It made no sense, but had knocked some sense into him…sufficient to discern the tightly wound frayed rope around the four cross members of the small steering wheel. He grabbed it with one hand, unrelentingly, and gave it a little tug…RD realized, miraculously at least one of the members of the couple were still clinging to life. He didn't know how much longer the ice would support his weight. He spread his appendages like a snow angel then waddled on all fours and slid the slippery bread pans toward him to displace his weight more evenly. He inched away from the frozen hole…the gateway to hell he imagined …and began to reel in his heavy treasure chest. He was careful not to wrap up and entangle the two in the soaked bed sheets. It took more than two to tango, and pull them to the surface. The dentist expelled his last breath and passed out due to LOC, loss of consciousness, his arms, rigor mortis presumably creeping in, still clutched around his sweetheart like a bear's paw around a pot of honey. He wouldn't surrender her to the other derelicts in Davy Jones' locker room…never! The tiny bubbles ascended then breached the surface; a reassuring sign for the seasoned warrior, that there was still some commotion down below. RD remained some distance from the edge of the relatively thick ice that had formed in a few days and waited….for what seemed like an eternity. Suddenly..a form lunged from the water. It sucked in a mouthful of the bitter icy air like a harp seal breaching the ice pack after being submerged past it's expiration time. The sub zero mixture stung his lungs…he choked and spat up the slushy surfactant ….then sucked in more of the miraculous mixture of oxygen, nitrogen and trace amounts of carbon dioxide and argon. His bride's tattered and torn black funerary rags clung to her body like seaweed. Had he sown the seeds of her destruction? In a desperate attempt he dragged her heavy lifeless form like a dead seal….over the snow to the flat aluminum pallet…RD had placed several layers of fur, his peace offering to trade at a remote Hudson's Bay trading post? Dr Gum peeled the wet icy rags from her body then shoved her inside the warm furry wrap, reminiscent of his earliest recollections of his mother's womb. He began to massage her breasts…heaving on her chest forcing the icy liquid from her lungs. She'd been under for at least 10 minutes, in her NDE state. Survivors of icy submersion in studies at Michigan and others had revived victims that were presumed, even pronounced dead down in the frigid waters longer than half an hour. The cryopreservative continued to circulate through her. Her metabolic rate and core body temperature had fallen deathly low.

"Rock…seeee, Rock…seeee" He refused to give up on her. He placed his frozen lips upon hers, hoping to inspire her. His icy exhalations entered her oral cavity and met considerable resistance. He expelled his entire tidal volume, heart and soul it seemed…then squeezed her midsection in an attempt to remove the icy crystals from her lungs.

"Come on, we have to hurry…back to the hotel!" The words echoed out over the lake..The haunting ring.. ripped through to his very soul. The death knell reverberated through his ear drums like a wild pounding war drum, a war from which no one returned. He looked over his shoulder at the imposing sinister obelisk…It sat there like a massive monument marking it's territory, a chilling cairn constructed from the building blocks, the very bones from all the victims that it had claimed over the years. It seemed to be smirking, waiting patiently for a few more…as long as it would take! RD threw a few furs over the trembling dentist… He still faced the harsh reality of freezing to death seemingly in the middle of nowhere… a burial at sea seemed so out of the question now…he'd rather die another day to face his demons in the hotel once again. He began to question his very sanity as he stared defiantly back at the sinister structure. RD resourcefully made a double sided winch with St Mary's Cox Comb as the pivotal point in the makeshift triangulated tether. He punched a hole in each bread pan, like the exit of an oil pan then secured the frayed knots to each sled. Around each of their waists he affixed another section of rope then fastened it to the central Cox Comb as well, four independent tethers. It formed a makeshift cross...and set of independent suspension for the wretched return trip to the inhospitable hotel. Dr Gum dreaded the thought yet knew in the back of his mind, there was no other alternative.

The porch light in front of Jebb's place, the meticulous meddler, the only undertaker around for miles. Either it had burnt out....since it had been burning since he left.. or his hopes of a double funeral service had been dashed with their rescue. The latter thought troubled him deeply. Perhaps all the town folk were in on some macabre ritual. Staying only in the event another unwary guest gathered enough gumption to endure a hellish holiday in the old hotel once more. He felt it was some sinister preordained, prearranged plan. He harbored and entertained several evil lingering notions as they made the perilous trek back to 'base camp'.. across the frozen flat tundra like wasteland. Running Deer did not like gambling with their lives, he simply carried out his task to

deliver them safely back to their outpost, like
some former excursion in the harsh outback..
Like Champlain or Cartier…they portaged,
carrying their heavy sleds or canoes and meager
rations…almost literally on their backs. The back
breaking ordeal in the brisk south winds that roared
through the narrow sluiceway, sliced at their
cheeks and exposed skin like a sharp razor.
Her lifeless lump…left him wondering if it were
not better to leave her here… incinerate her like the
night on marge of Lake Labarge they cremated
Sam McGee to conserve what little strength they
had left. The idea of a roaring fire, like their very
first night out at the Crypt lake trail head, appealed
to him. In lieu of the luxurious heat and hot lips
licking at his face he faced the harsh reality of a
hellish cold frisking him. The sharp porcupine
quills poked him…like a crazed acupuncturist.
It kept him on pins and needles, needless to say,
Just what the doctor ordered rather than a nauseous
mixture of nitrous oxide or stronger inhalation
anesthetic. He was certain she'd succumbed to
some form of the latter as he looked back…
calculating the distance they'd come thus far. RD

remained fixed on the prominent prize at the top of the hill. Several impediments and road blocks sat in their path. Several large protrusions, the erratic worn edges of the large boulders lay at the bottom of the steep cliffs; satisfied to wait for a feisty flight crew that sought to venture down the desolate fjord due to either misadventure, human error or simply a devil may care dare! Drinking and flying a deadly combination, as several victims had found out the hard way. Their pontoons smashed, their hopes dashed as they drowned a mere few meters away from the shoreline…as if sacrificed in a senseless gesture to appease the sacred structure high atop the mesa.

"Now for the fun part" predicted RD, as he methodically planned an ascent route. Base camp now presumably where they stood…the sacred ground of so many former victims.

"Raising the dead, with a little help from above?" Their goal the lofty pinnacle.. was just out of sight…perhaps the only saving grace. It gave them a few minutes to compose themselves, summon the last remaining ounces of strength and thank God…wherever he may be? Hopefully not missing in action! They were still very much alive so they knew he was hanging around somewhere nearby. The tired team looked directly ahead of themselves, focused on the first few steps. He'd have to crawl and learn to walk all over again it seemed as his weary legs buckled beneath him. Roxy strapped tightly to the sled, like a pretty little papoose in her maternal guardian's arms bounced and bobbed up and down…banging and clanging loudly over each large rock. If the fall hadn't killed her, the ascent certainly would! They clawed their way up the relenting soil buried beneath the snow pack, seemingly sliding back two feet for every one foot gained. Worse than the ascent of Ararat assumed the dentist, and amateur archaeologist. Enough wood to build at least a smaller rendition of Noah's Ark lay just over the next rise. Certainly enough kindling to have kept Noah's family alive for a few days coupled with a wiener roast atop the highest point, a peculiar flat plate or mesa… amongst the steep etched canyons, evidence of the perpetual grinding motion of the colossal sheets of ice that had slowly crept through the valleys down to the lake. The hotel only a much more recent addition to the charming rugged pristine terrain. They dared not stop and lose the valuable ground they'd gained like the offensive line in pursuit of the coveted Super Bowl trophy. Instead they dug into the side of the cliff, like an amnesic bear searching for it's former den…and with one last ditch effort dragged their butts toward the level playing field. Neither dared look back…he knew his young bride was still dragging him down, his beast of burden…likely…………. forever…

The eternal nubile noose dangled around his neck as he clawed his way over the edge. The garish guardian in all it's grandeur and splendor seemed to beckon them over the hump. The ghastly lights of the harbinger of doom, rather than a beloved light house …illuminated the fresh fallen snow eerily. The men boldly went where so many had gone before, but very few had left to tell of their trials and tribulations. They took a deep icy breath, both fearing they'd catch a deathly chill or pneumonia, then hurriedly dragged the body like two mindless headless horse back riders heaving a hearse carrying coffin, back inside the monstrous mausoleum.

RD undid the frayed knot then loosened the tight constricting rope from around his waist…and rushed to light a stove burner ASAP. The place was not much warmer than horrendous sub zero temperatures outside. RD reasoned the main boiler must've gone out..either due to an electrical short or simply the time elapsed since he had last tended to the mundane routine chore of feeding the beast. The only warmth was from the energy saving light bulbs emitting the dull orange reddish glow from the ghastly lampshades that remained lit. He'd have to hurry to avoid freezing to death now… The icy cold steel dials did not comply…they were frozen solid, they refused to rotate releasing the flammable fuel. He figured the gas lines had frozen as well…oh well he thought…they still had their large cavernous hearth in the center of the lobby if all else failed. But before he ventured into the deep dark recesses down stairs below the main floor; the place always gave him the creeps, steeped in sordid tales..of sinister spirits lurking about….he gave the massive ovens one more shot. In the meantime, with seconds now ticking away like the final countdown…Dr Gum had dragged his bride, certainly not the bookish type, but more burdensome than the heaviest book case speakers or book ends he'd ever hauled into any of his former significantly smaller residences. RD assisted to pull the sleigh through the Stallworthy dining room, in one swift swoop. A stall now may force them to leave her next to the window wondering what the sam hill…had happened in the last hour. The golden hour. Perhaps their finest effort of team work? They still had time to revive her as they laboriously lunged forward thrusting their torsos toward the massive rundle rock hearth. They were slipping into slumber…about to join his wife in the lame lifeless slumber party. RD dropped the frayed knots then headed across the lobby. He disappeared into the deep foreboding bowels of the building without a word or a trace.

Dr Gum frantically fumbled with the frayed knots….in a desperate attempt to free himself from the rope tightly wound around his…waist. He tossed the frayed section of slip knots aside…as he looked up into the lofty lobby and laughed…. ha, ha…thought you'd finished us off for good? did you eh? he deliberated in his mind, now in

deep thought; the disoriented deep recesses of
his mind still reeling from the death defying stunt,
he'd pulled. He pulled the warm soothing covers
of the large bear skin rug over Roxy….then
removed the last remnants of her tattered rags…
and threw them into the hearth. From rags to
riches? Or riches to rags? He knew not the rhyme
nor reason of the vicious cycle. They'd come full
circle. How they'd arrived back in the center of
their chilly accommodations…he couldn't care to
venture a guess. He peered long and hard into his
wife's lifeless eyes. He pressed his icy lips into
hers and began to exhale deeply into her closed
orifice.…perhaps it was the intoxicating effects of
the antifreeze still circulating in his system that
aroused her…from her sensual…suspended
animation like state, shrouded in evocative
memories and delicious dreams of decadent
behavior…a caged prisoner, powerless, overcome
by her captors…her animalistic instincts and urges
deeply aroused her…brought her back from the
borderline of death miraculously…as she slowly
responded. Her body thrust toward the source of
the heat. The hot heavy breath, and stench of

alcohol made her stir crazy, craving more of
the aromatic elixir…it had likely saved her life
…albeit she hadn't a care in the world in her
persistent sleepy state. As if teetering in the
nebulous netherlands, between sleep and fully
aware consciousness awoken after a thousand years
by her prince charming? She suddenly began to
gag…coughing, choking at the hands of her
assailant? She imagined a hideous heinous crime
…of depravity, debauchery, violating her, like
ravenous wolves or rabid dogs wanting their way
with her…She was suddenly equally repulsed by
the wretched stench of the booze that emanated,
gurgling from the ghoulish deathly pale grimace
that glared from on top of her.

She could only imagine what he'd conceivably
done to her. The devil himself by the pale moon
light like a ravenous obnoxious beast surely had
impregnated her…driven his seed deep inside her
aching loins. She coughed up some icy brackish
lake water…as if brought back from the dead or
edge of reason or some other erroneous suspended
cryogenic experiment gone terribly wrong. She
fought to remove the lecherous lout from on

top of her. She clawed, gnashed her teeth, like a rabid dog…furiously fighting for her freedom. He did not anticipate such a 'warm' welcome and resourcefully removed himself, rather extracted himself from under the folds of fur that enveloped her. Inspite of her resistance to the chilling remedy, he realized she had survived the ordeal.

9: Discovery

"I have made an important discovery
....that alcohol, taken in sufficient
quantities, produces all the effects
of intoxication."
                    - Oscar Wilde

The couple had been deprived of heat, other than their frigid torsos togetherness, teetering on rigor mortis now...for an eternity. Roxy still lay there in a daze, confused, not knowing exactly her state of mind nor could she feel her body. All the previous premonitions and clairsentient sensations certainly had come true. Whether she saw or felt her fingers were both gruesome revelations. Only her husband's palpations had pulled her through the trying ordeal. His adept course of action, the relentless CPR, and release of the preheated, albeit wretched reeking mixture into her mouth, was enough warmth to revive her. He enveloped her entire shivering, yet somewhat sensually aroused, abdomen and torso.

"Huh…. honey?" she pushed him off of her…seemingly coming to her senses….

"Bloomin' pity…" sighed RD as she slowly transformed into her irascible self. Roxy peered under the covers and although she could not feel her extremities, was slightly more relived to catch a glimpse of them….the polydactylism…alarmed her…so many fingers! Then finally realized the liquored lout was on top of her…probing, palpating every square inch of her frozen lifeless flesh like some crazed necrophiliac.

"I'll go turn up the heat" suggested RD, sensing it would be some time before they'd surface and attempt to start a fire. They were in no state to think coherently…still lost in a luxurious limbo land. As RD disappeared into the dark passageway to descend into the eerie depths, a dated dungeon like landscape surmised her husband, Roxy remarked,

"I'm beginning to simmer." Glad to see there is a faint glimmer of hope and the suggestion of even a small smile he said,

"You've got quite a frost 'bite' mark on your tush."

"Couldn't resist, could you?"

"From the fall."

"Fall?" She raised her head laboriously, from her prone position, sensing her rigid spine would snap. "It's the dead of winter!"

"Deader than you'll ever know." He was so grateful she began to find her bearings, from under the bare skin rug. At least some sense of time. They'd both taken a near fatal fall, miraculously extracted from the jaws of death by the resourceful medicine man.

"Wait a minute, was I? Were you…. on top?"

"You might say I was on 'top of things' " below the surface…but there was so much more he'd have to tell her in time. "although most of the debt of gratitude goes to RD." She was thoroughly confused by now…had she slept with both men? She was such a slut she surmised in her helpless provocative compromising position.

"Where is RD?"

He was glad she recognized his name, the next step was to familiarize herself with her immediate surroundings to see if she recognized the regal albeit wretched abode, the cause of all their calamity he assumed.

"He's gone to turn up the heat." The harsh reality of the situation slowly seemed to be coming back to her, how she'd slipped away in the nick of time, eluded her crazed captor, crept over the vast thin ice surface…only to crack through….the rest was a blur, a complete blank….other than a soothing warmth that radiated between both of their bodies.

"We don't need RD to turn it up a notch, do we?" She longing look into his bleary eyes, her hunger for him as she reached up to wrap her arms around his sore neck, was enough to sooth the savage beast. Unnerve him…as he raised his torso resisting her advance temporarily. Was she herself? Perhaps a little woozy from the fall?…His apprehension in her making a full recovery waned as he let gravity do the rest and slowly succumbed to her desires. His toned torso pressed into her shivering tired frame as if both had just endured a marathon run or bone crushing workout. Noticing their nakedness, she unabashedly became an explorer, rather than the enterprising economist she was in the chilly kitchen. The frozen chosen, selected for something more? in their mundane human existence were too weary and worn out to venture into a lengthy session of lovemaking. Their immediate presence and company was sufficient to set them at tranquility and ease as if after a long luxurious sexual encounter. They soon expired in each other's arms and slept for the few hours that remained of the moonlit night.

He arose shivering….in the frosty frozen lobby, looking around into the foyer and thought RD might have left the front door ajar. The palace was layered in a veil of permafrost…the window panes had received a frosty sparkling sheen…

"RD?" he yelled, then pecked his woman on the cheek. She was still dead to the world. He gently pried himself from her warm frame and reached for one of the terry cloth robes compliments of the

POW. RD must've left them he figured …confused why he hadn't fixed the boiler..or at least started a fire. The thought of freezing to death was foremost on his mind now. He rushed across the slippery surface of the lobby. It appeared the residents were planning to put a skating rink in the middle of the hotel. How odd. He slid into through the Stallworthy Dining room, out of control and rammed into a few draped tables. Rushing into the kitchen, he reached for the frozen dials, turned them all on, yet found little relief. Bleary eyed he saw what looked like a bloody red exudate oozing from the lebkuchen, German for 'living cake'? leber-liver, or liebe-meaning love, rather ironic he thought. A frightening foreboding omen indeed. Where was RD? There was no sign of their knowledgeable guide and life saver. Perhaps he was still in the bowels of the building fixing the boiler? It was definitely on the fritz as a deathly cold breeze blew in through the massive frozen aperture at the exit. The ice laiden particles suspended in a fine mist sailed up over the cliffs…swirling and dancing about in endless eddies from the regal impediment obstructing their cliff, then shot straight into the opening, the path of least resistance…

He decided to investigate and descend into the dark icy depths…He hoped he wouldn't find RD frozen to death, having fallen asleep trying to fix the decrepit furnace. "Mistakes are the portals of discovery" (James Joyce) he jested …reminding himself that 'stupidity kills', such a simple oversight if he were to see him frozen there like a totem pole…presumably pointing to the cause of the problem, yet powerless to procure a remedy. Some scant rays of light rebounded off the shiny frosty fixtures and foundations…like the means of illuminating the eerie inner passageways of an Egyptian pyramid leading to the burial chamber lying deep within. The stairwell opened into a cavernous boiler room which sat silently in the scarce light. Several shadows and silhouettes unhinged him. It was an eerie cold damp place… what one would expect to find in a medieval castle perhaps. The perfect place for an aspiring alchemist, to whip up his weird, potent concoctions …the crazy cure all albeit unproven remedies. Heaps of coal were piled up against the large broad mass of the boiler. It's large open orifice and two menacing portholes above the door on either side of the horseshoe shaped front facade stared like eyes … dating back to the time of the industrial revolution he estimated. It had belched out it's toxic nauseous fumes….Perhaps attributing to the flavor, aroma and overall ambience of the POW? The fumes…? the logical explanation, responsible for the persistent pipe smoke odor? The toxic mixture may have contributed to the macabre stories and rumors that floated around the place. Contributing to the madness and mystique of the menacing messages. They may have succumbed to some form of carbon monoxide poisoning ?…. rendering a temporary state of incoherence, perhaps even borderline insanity? His mind raced in a million directions…while his eyes darted methodically, slowly around the room. The few years of intense forensic science training came to the forefront. In the foreground, bones were scattered all about; they even leaned against the far walls, on the rickety old tables and counters…a few bottles and jars, potions from a previous mad scientist? Or all the indications of a shoddy amateur taxidermist? He checked the counter for a scratch scrip pad…not for his own ailments, but for a sign of RD's whereabouts.

"RD?"….No sign, no note, not a scrap of evidence he'd even been down to fix the furnace. He scoured through the brittle stale bones. They'd been shaven clean of cartilage, and gristle…likely even bleached, but could not detect a trace of it's pungent presence. His nostrils were practically chilled, covered in a thin, layer of permafrost…he chuckled. He was freezing his butt off; and had to hustle to complete his scan soon and get back up top in a desperate attempt to start a fire or face the consequences of conceivably freezing to death now. He took one last scan….around the dirty dinghy decrepit pit…. then picked up what he recognized to be the iliac bone of a buffalo or bison. The long thick smooth structure certainly supported a heavy hot headed mass…moving at a considerable speed over the plains…in a futile attempt to flee from it's assailants…there was no evidence of a struggle, a bullet hole, or scar, from a sharp arrowhead. The end must've come quickly …or inspite of all other possibilities..either ran to their deaths over 'Head Smashed in Buffalo Jump'…or simply died of old age..on the plains lying off the perimeter of the park. He found a few smaller bones by comparison, animal, perhaps grizzly bear or large brown bear? .. stacked in a macabre descending order…from largest perhaps to smallest species….wolf, coyote, down to rodent, raccoon…chipmunk…considering the region was rat free..perhaps Richardson ground squirrel or hotel mouse? ….the smallest but oft persistent peskiest presence…perusing the food stores and bags of rice, wheat, or flour and other rations…yet there was no form of sustenance in sight. It was arranged presumably by someone amused by collecting animal bones. An animal certainly did not have the dexterity, it's digits not capable of such complicated and precise form of artistic expression. He looked around for some lighter fuel, anything with which to start a fire, then stumbled over an odd projection deceptively concealed under the bones, the pile much smaller than he presumed. The boulder, perhaps an indigenous part of the infrastructure of the building like many of Frank Lloyd Wright's edifices, grown seemingly right out of the very rock and natural terrain. There were markings on it. His icy breath and brush strokes his frozen fingers, scratched the surface filling the musty space in a bony ashy cloudy mist. He coughed from the irritating nano particulate matter. The font, a former or extinct script perhaps; part of a Blackfoot sacred ritual? He studied it for a few seconds, it formed erratic trails of thought that seemed to make no sense, rhyme or reason…as they ran off the edge of the stone, unfinished?…it donned on him it may be something much more sinister, satanic…inscribed with incantations to summon the spirits of the dead… he knew the old alchemist's were searching for….

"A philosopher's stone?" a way to transmutate materials…an attempt to turn non precious metals into …….gold! a futile search for the elixir of life, the fountain of youth,

"White golden drops…"

Drunk to gain immortality….what the h… had been going on here? he questioned.

"The quintessence of life?"

Even the ancient Chinese emperors sought the

elusive elixir…as far back as the Ming dynasties. Many emperors and nobility succumbed to elixir poisoning, imbibing the bitter steeped blend of brew, oft laced with mercury and other toxic combinations.

"Immortali…tea?"

He shifted his attention to the counter…sifting though the stale putrid mist….then saw what looked like dried blood, dust and ash. The medical dental detective licked his finger than ran it over the filthy residue on the surface….then raised the sample to his lips…He licked the horrific bitter film from his fingertips…it left an awful ash taste. He scoped the counter for a glass, anything to wash away the God awful lingering taste. It was then that he noticed the shards of fine 'bone china'…in various stages of fabrication? Small fine camel hair brushes…the pieces of the perplexing puzzle began to fall into place.

"A peculiar porcelain procuring process?" he postulated in shock and awe. Not the alchemist's experiments he had assumed at all as he gazed along the bench. It was then that he spotted a few more bones….not the bovine, buffalo or porcine variant. He slowly went to pick one up to feel it's distinct protuberances…He couldn't fathom what he found.. an actual human bone. He examined it's weathered exterior surface. There were no immediate tell tale marks, no signs of a struggle; no blunt force trauma, or sharp penetrating wounds …injection or aspiration points. He peered around, stacked amongst the animal collection were indeed more human bones…that led to a cold brick façade .. a row of grim reminders of what may have transpired in the town. Wutherington's dirty little secret? The 'elixir of life'? the chef's poison of choice to intoxicate his lovely wife…? When all else failed….'death by chocolate', or fatal drowning, deadly decapitation ….the deadly brew delivering the knock out punch…then disposing of the evidence in the dark diabolical laboratory? incinerated, incorporated in the exquisite tea service sets? What a sinister secret! His mind could wrap around the gruesome murder method…it only grew some more as he felt the comparatively warm wall.. The mason must've made a secret chamber...a bizarre burial vault behind or within the existing foundation much like the secret chambers concealed in the Egyptian tombs…perhaps that's where the chef buried his wife's bones? Her final resting place? A continuous endless supply of skeletal remains to supply the craftsmen…working alone or in teams of highly trained henchmen to carry out the macabre manufacturing process? It made no sense other than to satisfy a cruel craving for some sinister coven's spiritual ritual…something much more macabre than any native medicine chant or dance he imagined existed. This delved into the very depths of disturbed demonic devices. The dark gory satanic mills referred to by musicians in the days of yore…He was appalled at what had been conceivably going on behind closed doors for nearly a century. It left him with a sick putrid feeling in the pit of his stomach.

"Lovely little palace you've got here prince. A place of love potions, torture, devil worship?" He dared not let his imagination conjure up and …. delve into the sordid details.. the macabre methods of deliverance…the helpless prey, preyed upon by something much more sinister than a few foolish ghosts playing a few pranks inside the elegant exterior. The fanciful façade of the regal residence held a dark sinister secret indeed! What he needed now was a stiff drink! The word stiff resonated; rebounded in his cranium…like an errant stray bullet….aimed to put him out of his misery or driven to pull the trigger at the hands of his own device to drive out the demons that were brought to bear on each subsequent guest…They all entered at their own risk, entertained, amused by the a few ghostly stories in the 7 story structure. Their ultimate fate he figured all came to a 'bitter' end.. perhaps over tea and crumpets in the Valley View Dining room or lapping a luxurious Bailey's Irish Cream in the Weeping Willow Lounge? …the final act and closing chapter culminating in a cruel culling ritual. Ranting, raving, repeating the demonic passages; roasting the guests, perhaps even while still alive, finally sealing their fate…in the burial chamber…the crypt…such a sordid tall tale. It was why no one ever truly left the premises he presumed… their fond memories, the talk of the town…over tea. Such a delightfully devilishly delicious way to spend an afternoon. A truly original 'Tale from the Crypt' originating in the very town of Wutherington itself. MADE IN WUTHERINGTON, had his curiosity piqued. It left him spellbound. First and foremost on his mind now was to get out….as far and fast as he could. Save his wife any way he could think of…. before the inherent nature of the haunted hotel had it's way and naturally took it's course…

He hurried to dash up the stairs but tripped over more brittle bones.. It bothered him, unhinged him…as he pushed himself up from the dusty human debris…how many others? How many distinguished guests had disappeared over the years? Unbelievable as it seemed…the sinister sequence of events made perfect sense! He felt a dusty volume just beyond his fingertips as he spread them to push himself off the dusty stone surface. He expelled a burst of air like a bellow fanning the flames in a hearth. A guest book he wondered? All the unwary weary travelers that had signed away their souls? By leaving their signature in the guest registry…for ever etched in the book of life? Or death depending upon the manager's desires? The POW's own demonic way to honor it's guests in one final hellish gruesome toast

…over tea and crumpets?

"Mutus Leber"…he recognized the writing…the Latin inscription…lingered in his library like mind …letting the words decipher themselves…the detective delved into the virtual dewey decimal system deliberating….deciding which row of volumes to hoe. He came to the Latin section.

"Latin ..uh…."…meaning "silent book" he remembered. Medical, mystical literature…. Apothecaries…carrying out formulations.. dating back to Isaac Ballot from France in the 1600's… for manufacturing …the philosopher's stone! He flipped through the flimsy parched pages …shocked by the sparse strange few illustrations. He counted fifteen in total. Medieval? native lore mixed in? He couldn't make it out. No matter, he'd use it for kindling…as he crept up the stairs… he turned around one last time…to dispel the possibility that his over active imagination hadn't conjured up the unbelievable image. Or the possibility that in his inebriated state, he'd slipped into his deep dark subconscious much further than he preferred. The vast catacombs of his mind that kept all the sordid secrets, the macabre thoughts highly guarded in the vault…had somehow surfaced, and crept into the realm of reality. He feared the fumes and toxic stench had a part to play in the particularly disturbing discovery.

"Brrrr…." He shivered. The palace was a bloody ice bucket…he peered around..No newspapers, no paper napkins, nothing with which to start a fire. No brochures in the gift shop. He ran to the front desk, not a guest book or registry, no notes, no itinerary….not a scrap of paper! He ran into the Stallworthy dining room…no paper serviettes… no Kleenex?…what kind of an inhospitable place was this? Certainly stripped to the bare bones in the off season! He didn't want to dwell on the last thought All he noticed were boxes and boxes of cardboard boxes marked 'BONE CHINA'…. 'MADE IN WUTHERINGTON'! It didn't don on the buffoon, immediately still immersed in the incredible insights he'd made just below the surface of the main foyer the answer to his problems lay right in front of his face! There was sufficient cardboard to kindle a festival of lights he discovered as he began to tear them apart….leaving the stacks of exquisite tea sets stacked precariously, teetering on the slippery surface of the frozen floor....he was one of the frozen chosen he figured, refusing to cede to the seedy sinister hotel. He continued to tear the strips from the boxes...as the former taxidermist may have ripped the rancid strips of flesh off his unfortunate forlorn victims...like some crazed creature turned to cannibalism like the Chilean soccer team during their tragic ordeal to survive stranded in the after math of the fatal plane crash...The math didn't add up. Of the 45 passengers and flight crew of Uruguayan AF Flight 571...several were sucked out of the severed fuselage as it struck the tips of the Andean summit. Several more quickly died due to their injuries or succumbed to the bitter cold and froze to death. 8 died in an avalanche that swept through their makeshift shelter in the hollowed out fuselage. The few survivors faced with certain starvation, turned to feasting on their fellow passengers to survive. Search and rescue teams did not learn of the tragedy for some 72 days after two hardy souls trekked for 12 days over the treacherous terrain to alert the authorities. In total 16 passengers miraculously emerged from the Fairchild FH

227-D wreckage. The grim reminder gnawed at his guts. Faced with the grim prospect of devouring each other…he placed their chances at slim to nil. The ordeal had already taken it's toll on his wife's trim former fashion model frame. She'd become a complete mental and emotional wreck if he divulged the fact that their chances of getting out alive were fading with each fleeting breath that she took. It only compounded the problems as he pounded his fist on the frozen counter….eyeing the endless array of stacked porcelain plates…and one ever present wretched awful reminder…the frosty bloody POW caricature, the evil persona preserved in the gruesome presentation, it's insatiable craving to crush and devour the poor souls who happened to venture into the awful accommodations during the off season.

Roxy began to stir. Her bleary watery bloodshot eyes were still sealed shut. Either from peering from the furry cozy covers into the chilly frozen foyer, or still hung over? She couldn't determine which was which. Must've been some party she figured, trying to pull herself together. She probed around trying to establish some sense of her

surroundings and tactile sensation and regain
her bearings. Roxy ran her fingers over the furry
covering.. of her husband's pajamas? Her hand
slowly probed the protuberance near her face like a
Braille decoder. She soon recognized the bony
protuberance before her.. two eyes, a shiny glossy
nose and a massive mouth, something very
menacing. Her fingers found two large long sharp
canines to confirm her suspicion.

"My what big canines you have. Did you have
your teeth capped, dear?" She inserted her finger
into the creature's mouth…the tongue was not
moist or mobile like her husbands… "Honey?"
She lowered the covers…then instantly emitted
a blood curdling scream. With super human
strength, she grabbed the gruesome horrible
grimace and threw the entity off her chest… the
ursus horribilus was indeed dead.. the wretched
rug…remained right next to the hearth…eyeing her
every move. She sat up fully awake, stirred to her
senses. Roxy realized rather embarrassed, her
torso, her top half was completely uncovered. She
shivered uncontrollably then quickly concealed
her nakedness and scooted under cover of the

furry folds.

Her husband dashed into the decrepit lobby.. the land of the living dead albeit grateful for any sign of life from his beloved bewildered bride.

"It's a miracle, you're alive!"

He rushed toward her to comfort her…She didn't recognize him at first, resisting his advances still very disoriented. His flushing bride fought his friendly charming chair, er rather bed side manner of approach. Had the fiend tried to kill her? She couldn't think clearly, confusion sunk into the crevices of her cold cranium.

"Stop right there…before you go any further" she urged her aggressive assailant. The lyrics reverberated in her mind. A macabre reminder? Meat loaf…something to leave a lasting impression with the gala dinner guests…had the persistent chef indeed preserved his precious wife within? As part of the secret ingredients of the non vegetarian ghoulash? The ghastly grim guest list…more than menu items, but the actual menu itself? The green thumbs gathered in the 'soylent green'…human hamburger helper. She couldn't help herself and began to wheeze and cough…perhaps the onset of pneumonia or pertussis? The gut reaction was an instant physiological response to the possibility of the sinister food preparation practices engaged in by the seemingly well coached sous chef! Her imagination ran away with her again ….running wild and uninhibited as she imagined she might have last night as she peered around her icy surroundings. Where was she? conceivably in the 'ice hotel' in Scandinavia? The lobby had become a sheet of ice…the walls had a frosty while film on them, concealing the ornate woodwork underneath. How did she get here she wondered? And who was this energetic frisky little elf trying to fondle her? Olaf? Or some other mischievous mythical Norse trouble maker? She was beside herself…then blurted out of the blue…albeit even her fingers were turning blue from lack of heat and food.

"Did we…?"

She didn't wait for answer as she quickly threw the covers over her…as if she'd seen a ghost. Her husband an even more gruesome grim reminder of the carnage, pillaging and plundering that must've occurred in the palace last night! Yet she had no recollection whatsoever of what had taken place!

"Rock…seee…it's meee." As he held his hands to his chest like a wild beast about to bellow out a bloodcurdling scream…a baboon in heat? Huh? about to let loose, foot loose and fancy free to roam around the ramparts…What on earth was going on? Had the earth been over run by apes in the aftermath of a nuclear holocaust? Now nothing but a frozen wasteland? Her vivid imagination evaded the obvious, the most logical answer to her nagging dilemma.

She noticed the fool holding reams of cardboard strips? Que pasa? He was either demented or meant to start a fire…was there no paper? And as great minds often think alike he uttered,

"Hotel going paperless…impossible. No TP?" she wondered…she was sure he checked it while she kept the wigwam warm… He tossed the cardboard entrails then trekked back into the kitchen for more kindling.. She came up with an idea as she peered over to the old player piano in the opposite side of the entertainment center.

The tall ornate player piano stood like an silent overgrown coffin anticipating a late arrival, guests that never came to the gala suarrey? She was rather disappointed that the place had fallen into utter disrepair …but realized there might be reams of paper inside …rather than a rotting body as she came to her senses. In a trance like state she wrapped the POW terry cloth robe around her and rushed to the dusty idle keyboard…Roxy stood before it; and rather than reach inside to search for a scrap of paper…she sat down and began to play. Her fingers danced over the icy ivory…Dr Gum was dumbfounded as he discovered the source of the inspiring sounds. Rather than a rotting roll of paper…..

10: Angels and Demons

> "An artist is a creature driven by
> demons. He doesn't know why they
> chose him and he's usually too busy to
> wonder why."
>   - William Faulkner

"A rising star, who knew? You never cease to amaze me."

The dentist circled his wife in a wide circle heading straight for the Weeping Willow lounge to grab a couple bottles of whiskey, rum or whatever was available. Now, not only to start a flaming fire but dispel any preconceived notions he harbored about his wife's countless latent talents.

Her ability to encompass the entire keyboard in a disconcerting concerto stunned even her. Her ears and eyes watched in amazement as her hands rattled off an entire verse of

"Resurrection" by Gustav Mahler's symphony in #2 in C major. she replied in an unusual utterance …her angelic voice and demeanor did not mean to offend or alarm him…..as she playfully performed the player piano roll favorite. The haunting melody reverberated throughout the chilly acoustic chamber….

> Rise again, yes rise again
> Will you my dust
> After a brief rest
> Immortal life..immortal life
> Will he who called you, give you
> To bloom again were you sown!
> The Lord of the harvest goes
> And gathers in, like sheaves,
> Us together, who died.

He sat at the bar and poured himself a long stiff drink, debating whether to drown his sorrows forgetting about the fire altogether as he listened to the haunting albeit heart warming tune. Had she passed on into a parallel plain of existence, permitting her precocious abilities to surface. A prodigy in a former life or parallel universe…or perhaps a result of the military experiments meddling in her mental abilities through mind control…Countless theories surfaced…as she played a perfectly flawless symphony. She certainly wasn't herself since the 'baptism', the immersion in the icy bath….brought back from the dead…to deliver this macabre albeit melodic message? Her calm composed upright profile left him in a quandary. A perfect image, of her former forlorn self, why the sudden surge in energy? Had she become a medium or demon in disguise? Playing him for a fool…to deliver him to….

He was overcome with rage….he had to drive out the demons….he found a pack of POW matches… behind the bar, relatively dry, still potentially able to achieve his aim. He beelined for the giant hearth uncertain of what she'd do next? Not knowing if she'd deal a fateful blow with one swift swoop of her delicate digits. It was the booze talking now he assumed as he fumbled with the folds on the pack of matches to expose the last fleeting opportunity to return the cavernous space to room temperature. She turned toward him, twisting her neck noticeably more than expected. Even he could sense her limber spine begin to snap.

"Last of the Mohecans?" she laughed, in a hideous cackle that accompanied the tune in a most peculiar way. "The last boy scout you're not!" He paused to ruminate over her words as the pack of matches burst into flames. The deceptive heat singed his fingertips. He dropped the flaming torch.. momentatily stunned, then kicked it in the general direction of the hearth….the cardboard strips that he'd arranged into a makeshift teepee remained unlit. He quickly poured a trail of 80 proof rum onto the top of the structure…which seemed to spontaneously burst into flames….
He leapt back from fright…in the nick of time …avoiding an intense hot facial. The flames slowly rose…in the huge hearth. The icy draft quickly sucked the life out of the fire. He hurried to toss more cardboard kindling onto the toppling tepee… Then pulled the cork off a bottle of Chablis ….taking a small sip, satisfied, he sequestered his desire to get drunk…and focused his attention

on simply stayin' alive. He took one last long look at the macabre medical apothecary manuscript the parched pages could complement the cause, he felt...he held the 'Mutus Liber', the Book of Silence'...damned the writers. "Publishers are demons, there's no doubt about it" then tossed it onto the fire....the flames engulfed the highly contentious flammable material, fuel for thought... and turned to his beloved....fixated on the fire...The flames danced in her pupils.

"Ich liebe dich" he said softly in a contemplative trance. "Translated from the German, 'I love you' from the Hebrew leb meaning inner man, spirit, soul, conscience...he looked across the lobby lovingly at his bride then untwisted the top off another bottle of JD- Jack Daniel's whiskey....then deliberated like a doctor of jurisprudence, and a compelling double edged sword opening statement,

"My water of life" then downed a heavy dose of the strong medicinal elixir. "My reason to live".... She was puzzled by the remark...speechless for a few moments, uncertain if he meant her...to love and hold in his hearth forever or his intoxicating elixir...destined to forever remain a prisoner of it's vile vices. She feared he'd soon turn into a recurring possessed demon impassioned by the potent poison. He doused the alchemist's manual ….slowly consumed in the fire…dispelling any lingering doubt she had. It burst into a dazzling display that exploded with a loud crackle like a cleverly crafted magician's trick. He poked the fire with a long icy iron that hung by the hearth. The metal warmed his hand…soon a searing heat as he lost track of time as his wife walked his way toying with the chord of her terry cloth robe…The radiant reflection of the flames on her former pale complexion seemed to revive her. It confused him, arousing him to his very core. She sauntered seductively his way…wearing only the robe, which now hung loosely over her statuesque shoulders… She was playing him again…for a fool? As she approached the fire. His angelic creature seemed aroused by the fire as well.. It rejuvenated her animalistic cravings it seemed… lost in a trance she slowly knelt by the rising flames….It's soothing warmth enveloped her, holding her, caressing her…as she swooned and swayed …slowly from side to side…he observed her swaying hips and torso, entranced by her presence, his pretty little Polynesian private dancer. He savored her dramatic display of song and dance imagining the angelic voice that may emerge from her throat. Her present state a pleasant surprise. He lapped it up as she had his redundant mundane lectures and deliberations. As he gently touched her, she shook, taking a sudden turn for the worse. Overwhelmed by the aura that accompanied his touch, a chilly recurring clairsentience set in. The sudden mood swing and her unexpected response forced him to back away. She began to hum a haunting melody…the steady beat in her voice emanated through her body…defiantly forsaking her former serene self. Her lips burst out a bizarre powerful rendition of a popular song she'd heard on the radio, presumably prior to their departure…

> "This used to be a funhouse
>
> now it's filled with evil clowns
>
> It's time to start the countdown
>
> I'm gonna burn it down…
>
> (Pink, Funhouse lyrics)

He was beside himself….as he watched her smash several bottles into the blazing inferno…

Fearing she may burst into flames from the proximity to the deceptively hot blaze, he pulled her hurriedly away. She resisted his advance, suddenly struck with an overwhelming sense of an evil entity again. Her torso rose in a total trance, in a rhythmic erratic swivel, not that of a gently swaying hula dancer but a defiant feisty punk rocker as he tried to label her movements.

> 'I dance around this empty house
>
> tear us down, throw you out
>
> screaming down the halls
>
> spinning all around now we fall

Her recollections of the past weeks, in interpretive song and dance disturbed him. She'd reacted in a rather unexpected uncharacteristic rebellious manner. He didn't realize the ramifications of his actions. Perhaps unaware of his antics due to the incessant alcoholic binges and black outs…

> Pictures framing up the past
>
> Your taunting smirk behind the glass
>
> This museum full of ash
>
> Once a tickle, now a rash…

He was stunned by her omnipotent vivid awareness of the world that lay underneath the dance floor;

she'd never visited the vacuous vault of human depravity he thought.. He couldn't venture a guess as to when she may have slipped downstairs…

> This used to be a funhouse
> But now it's full of evil clowns
> It's time to start the countdown
> I'm gonna burn it down, down, down
> I'm gonna burn it down.
> 9,8,7,6,5,4,3,2,1,fun

She was enraptured in herself.. spinning wildly around…looking up into the lofty icy lobby….
He assumed she savored their sweet sexual antics in the Lakeview Suite…yet sensed something much more sinister in her raspy deep voice.
She did not even once acknowledge his presence or look in his direction as she deliberated her intentions. She simply continued to spin as if possessed. Her mad gyrations soon sending her into a tailspin he sensed… ever ready to catch her in his waiting arms….

> Echoes knocking on locked doors
> All the laugher from before
> I'd rather live out on the street
> Than in this haunted memory.

He became rather alarmed at her perceptive albeit disturbing rant.

> I've called the movers called the maids
>
> We'll try to exorcise this place
>
> Drag my mattress to the yard
>
> Crumble tumble house of cards

He was thoroughly confused by her phrases, another premonition. What on earth was happening to her, and what was she planning?

> This used to be a funhouse
>
> But now it's full of evil clowns
>
> It's time to start the countdown
>
> I'm gonna burn it down, down, down
>
> 9,8,7,6,5,4,3,2,1, fun

He knew an entity possessed her..something sinister…consuming her, compelling to act so out of character. The rebellious rabble rouser…aroused by the flames…rising higher and higher….She grabbed a few more full bottles from the stocked source. The Weeping Willow may fuel the fire for some time.. yet feared they'd deplete their only source of heat in a jiffy. They'd still freeze to death if they didn't pace themselves. He pulled her aside …and flung her onto the floor. She slowly

assumed a doggy style position…arched her
back and panted like a lap dog…He didn't know
what to expect next as she finished her verse.

> I'm crawling through the doggy door
>
> My key don't fit my life no more
>
> I'll change the drapes, break the plates
>
> I'll find a new place,
>
> burn this sucker down!
>
> Do, do, do, do, do, do, do
>
> Do, do, do, do, do, do, do
>
> This used to be a funhouse
>
> But now it's full of evil clowns
>
> It's time to start the countdown
>
> I'm gonna burn it down, down, down
>
> I'm gonna burn it down.

The disconcerting, haunting lyrics left him
spellbound. What was she referring to? He peered
up into the rafters…clowns plural….the perplexing
phrase. If she referred to only him, her clown, he'd
understand; but several clowns…curdled his
stomach… her earlier references to an exorcism…
left him lost in thought…in despair…dire straights.
His marriage certainly on the rocks now…
He snapped out of it seeing the slowly dying

embers…in the hearth as it rapidly exhaled it and carried out of the chilly chamber of horrors. He had to keep it burning…as his bride bolted about on all fours, like a crazy demonic cat or rabid dog, he quickly grabbed a couple chairs and dragged them toward the hearth. He peered around in a mad daze…disoriented…spinning around rapidly. She didn't know if he was emulating her in a loving albeit macabre manner. He desperately sought the implement to provide an eternal source of heat. He dashed into the kitchen. A cold icy breeze came in from the disengaged unhinged 'doggy door'. He knew he'd have to hurry. He found the razor sharp axe,,, then ran back into the lobby with a crazed demented look on his face… Roxy raised her arms in a desperate futile attempt to thwart her assailant…he raced by her…She thoroughly confused, fell to the floor sighing in relief. He raised the axe high over his head…then purged his pent up energy coupled with his emotional unrest and unleashed a hideous howl as if summoning the demons from hell. Roxy covered her ears in disgust at the total disregard for the ambience and enhanced acoustics in the hellishly

cold auditorium. He hacked one of the high
back chairs to pieces with a couple swings of the
sharp implement, then tossed several slivers into
the fire… the flames leapt in appreciation,
appeasing the persistent craving for more firewood.
He grabbed several more sections of furniture in a
mad frenzy; she jumped out of his way, fearful
he'd inadvertently dismember her and toss her
limbs into the inferno….added to his collection, as
if sorting the wheat from the chaff like a demented
interior designer , there appeared to be no method
to his madness….yet from the lofty lobby
balconies the virtual audience…viewed the
unfolding drama fully comprehending the scene.
The final act, to deliberate and deliver them both
to the deeply rooted evil spiritual presence
adjudicating the performance? For high above in
the upper ramparts, the odd arrangement of
furniture, not the neat and tidy tiny enclaves,
seemed to spell the sinister recurring phrase….

K I L L R O X Y

Completely foreign to the mad furniture mover
and his forlorn assistant sitting a safe distance
away…Mere pawns in the passionate play

choreographed by the puppet master? The ever present evil eye witness to the travesties and sinister shenanigans that had carried on in the hallowed halls for nearly a century....was amused. In a feverish frenzy, he forcefully whittled away years of painstakingly fine craftsmanship and attention to detail. The exhausting exercise took but a few mere hour...the golden hour...certainly not the hotel's finest hour. The regal residence slowly fell into utter disrepair, as if noticeably neglected. The notorious logger left little to the imagination like the grim reaper, come to gather his harvest in the gruesome mess. The former glory of the elegant façade gone. All that remained were the ghostly guests and staff from the past. The current occupants from opposite ends of the spectrum appeared as either homeless vagabonds camping out in the inhospitable unheated hacienda or rambunctious rock stars... resolved to raising the roof by their rantings and ravings and raising cane...chopping the colossal structure to wood chips.... They were chips off the old block. Roxy's attention always anxiously averted to him for she didn't know when he'd turn the axe on her..in mad

frenzy mistaking her bare skin, human legs
and arms for fancy legs and armrests of an elegant
Victorian high back leather chair that leaned
against the other pile of rubble. The wild workout,
the fiery look in his eyes, fueled by the sheer
instinct to survive…ceded to a calmness, a
composed sensibility she sensed. The demonic
demented dentist, aspiring author bound for an
insane asylum or whatever role he'd played prior to
the intense purging…relieved her. He seemed to
return to his former self…. as he sat for a few
seconds to catch his second wind. The warm
blazing fire roared, now the sole source of sound
and heat in the haughty hotel. It seemed to purge
the demons that resided within both of them. The
two were emotionally, physically and mentally
drained from their ordeal…determined in their
desperate attempt to stay alive. to stay alive…
as long as a source of fuel remained. He'd topple
the tall timbers that held the palace together he
declared, if he had to …destined to drive out the
very demons that lurked in the lobby, the
balconies, the wretched rooms, every nook and
cranny of the colossal demonic pit. He'd ride out

the storm, as he slowly came back to his senses, with his wife by his side. The furniture slowly whittled away…the message was loud and clear, not to themselves but the inherent insane inhabitants, the persistent pranksters…the writing was on the wall and in the engravings in the lobby..

I L L R O X Y

The demonic desire to eliminate his enchanting companion ceased, replaced with an equally energetic urgency to unravel their dire dilemma and drive the demons out hopefully forever. Were they both still heavily sedated? Still comfortably cushioned by the copious amounts of anti freeze circulating through their bloodstream. Their self medicated regimen, the heavily dispensed pain killers eased their wretchedly sore aching muscles. Yet the progressively almost imperceptibly smaller doses of the luxurious liquor due to the high demand of the raging roaring fire brought them slowly back to their senses. The psycho babble brought on by the booze, abated. The prescription for a safe and sound recovery practically wrote itself….

I L L R X

The best medicine…their insidious sinister thoughts turned to loud laughter as if to purge the demons from their humble abode. The same entities that had nearly driven them to suicide or murder mitigated as their satiated synaptic endings ceased to fire, imperceptably impeded through the slow steady imbibition of the elixir of life. It slowed their furious frenzy to a snail's pace. Roxy erupted into a rousing roaring round of laughter as she stared at the buffoon….A giddy glow grew on her face. The fool toasted to her health…then tossed the contents of the half full bottle onto the blazing fire.

"The cost of heating this place is driving me to drink" he declared…then proceeded to seat himself in mid air…in a game of macabre musical chairs, now missing…from the formula and stumbled to the floor. The propensity to feel any pain in his posterior as he hit the floor eluded him in his heavily self medicated state. Roxy continued to chuckle at the crazy clown's antics… One down,,, how many more lecherous lunatics lurked in the lobby? as she looked around. She tried to recall the reason why she'd acted the way she did, what had come over her, as a soothing warmth enveloped her…like an angelic presence. A heavenly harbinger of hope? Her husband apprehensively reached out to her to wrap his arms around her…Her defenses seemingly down in the surreal false sense of security, her safety net or blanket, the menacing grizzly bear skin rug… now lay next to the hearth at a safe distance. He decided to take one more stab at holding her. He desperately sought her soft smooth skin alarmed by the fact his angel allowed him to hold her. A lingering thought penetrated is cool calm exterior. The ever present palatial space continued to close in on them.

"Do you think we'll ever get out of here?" she sighed softly during their brief lapse of sanity …sanilocity? The travel agency they should've booked their holiday with? he laughed…He was lost in limbo, turning the pages of the past, preferring to focus on the future. He had to summon all his cunning crafty creativity to concoct a way to get the hell out of the hotel, once and for all. The fire would eventually burn itself out… As long as the thermostat was turned up, he took

the opportunity to dwell on their ordeal...
How they'd evaded death....so much food for
thought...he extracted himself delicately from her
then strolled over to the massive dense desk. In the
event of an emergency or if the fire conceivably
went out, he'd chop his writing desk into tiny tooth
picks...and resort to writing the last chapter on the
floor. Or allow the ghost writer to pen the final
passages...as he stared off into space. Only the
crackling soothing fire emanated in the vast
vacuous vault. They'd come full circle indeed,
rather odd, ending up nestled by a roaring campfire
at the 'Grand Hotel'...eerie recollections of the
haunting Deep Purple lyrics...from the song
'Smoke on the Water' filled his fertile mind. His
overactive imagination cast a careful watchful eye
on the flames as it continued to spit and belch out
exploding embers. Perhaps it was simply the calm
before the real chaotic storm? The CHAOS card
came to mind, nagging him, nudging him to stay
awake...a fire still first and foremost on his mind.
He flipped the switch on the laptop to jot a few
points, but found the power had gone off. Only the
radiant ghostly glow from the fire served to

enlighten the forlorn look on their faces. His stomach growled loudly, disturbing the peaceful silence; a menacing reminder. They weren't out of the woods yet. In all the excitement they'd forgotten to thaw out a few basic food stuffs and preserves. He excused himself to rush into the ice box…beyond the perimeter of the radiant heat from the hearth. The kitchen lay in utter disarray. The frosty icy fingers crept across the counters greedily grabbing whatever warmth and rations remained. The temperature difference between inside and outside of the fridge and freezer seemed indeterminable. He desperately sought RD's advice. Perhaps he knew of some ancient Indian secret to survive the bitter cold winter from within a rising tapering tepee? How did they do it? The thought assured him they'd make it.. provided they stay close to the roaring campfire. To hell with the rest of the wretched hotel. Where was the seasoned medicine man he wondered. He peered out over the anything but enchanted bay…recalling their hideous ordeal. Utter darkness had descended on the town of Wutherington. No harbor lights highlighted the boathouse.

Roxy tiptoed into the culinary lab, tightly wrapped in the POW terry cloth robe. It had become a chilly chamber of horrors. The mini gingerbread hotel continued to seep blood ominously. She knew the nightmare was anything but over. Broken porcelain plates and sharp shards were strewn everywhere…she envisioned a veritable food fight to the death, as she stepped cautiously, concerned not to slide…on the slippery icy surface.. a careless accident could still spell the death of them both…

"We're never going to get out of here, are we? The POW won't let us leave?" she worried as she peered across the lake. The heavy fresh snowfall had made passage practically impossible. An impenetrable fortress sat on top of the prominent point…probably 'til spring she feared as she peered at their meager 'frozen TV dinner' rations. Why, she couldn't even locate a green tea bag in the midst of the mountainous stacks of porcelain saucers. She'd even settle for a 'black ' Japanese Kombucha, now. There was some sort of strange macabre irony in it all. As if the ghost writer of the POW was still in command, cunning, conniving, carefully calculating the final chapter of her husband's best seller. Perhaps he'd only reap the rewards post humously?...The royalties relinquished to a trust fund in the name of the manager of the POW or former resident...The wretched thought crept into her consciousness... She shuddered at the ominous notion.

"Bloomin' pity?"

"Immortali...tea?" he questioned...as if reading her mind.

11: Last Resort

"Every man is his own doctor of divinity
in the last resort."
- Robert Louis Stevenson

He peered around the frozen wasteland or
shattered dreams and decrepit desserts.

The distraught dentist…transformed into the
decadent chef that he'd become…knew this may
be their last chance, ditch effort to dine then
hopefully dash from the inhospitable hotel. He held
her tight; the prospect of leaving her or losing her
to the apparitions in the abode, an insane asylum,
set his mind in motion. The dedicated DDS, doctor

of dental surgery, meant nothing more than the 'dread of dining solo' he realized…the wretched culinary operatory of former dismembered staff and spouses likely drugged, dragged to their deaths, down into the dark bowels of the abode to appease the beast. It left a queasy feeling in the cavernous pit of his stomach. How could anyone have stooped to such depths? Totally deprived of human decency, depraved, deluded, driven by their own demons and hallucinations…he wished he'd opted for the DDV degree now. The coveted doctor of divinity to drive the demons from the decrepit residence….an exercise in futility now, to exorcise any evil spirits demanded substantial spiritual stamina. His coffers were tapped as were hers. He was running on empty…his famished overworked mind, simply slipping into overdrive?….destined to drive them both mad.

"Where the devil is RD?"

He wondered where Running Deer was, conveniently eliminated from the equation once again. Never around when he was needed. Perhaps he was the perpetrator, the prankster? A permanent fixture to preserve the lore and mystique of the macabre mansion on the mesa…

He refused to cede to the persistent notion that they'd never get out….

"I decline to accept the end of man." (William Faulkner) he stated defiantly…nor woman for that matter. What mattered, was to make the most of a rapidly deteriorating bad situation. He rushed back into the lobby with her to keep an eye on the crackling fire.. at this moment their only hope of outlasting the nightmarish ordeal. Not one to waste his words, other than in a passionate stemwinder, or heated argument over the merits of some new medical miracle or promising pharmacautical; more action he told himself as he paced back and forth in front of the hearth. His compassionate loving, caring, copilot, now seemingly the only source of inspiration…she had miraculously survived the frightening uncharted flight plan, and stood by his side through it all.

"Politics are a lousy way for a man to get things done. Politics, like God's infinite mercy, are a last resort" he recalled, preferring to set his plan into action. Either one of them or both of them would eventually have to leave to get help he figured.

Remaining here in the bulbous burnt out fuselage, a veritable C130 Hercules, he reckoned or like languishing inside the belly of the beast, a monstrous mammal, a beached whale....spelled certain disaster and death. He didn't believe anyone would bother to come look for them 'til spring anyway. Why, no one even knew they were here. His secret clandestine desire to get away with her on the romantic tryst had turned into a desperate attempt to reconnect and communicate with the outside world. No radio, no TV, nor way to trek out of the treacherous terrain, entirely surrounded in a surreal entrapment brought upon by his foolish flight of fancy to finish the novel essentially removed from the free world. The bitter irony floored him, the POW of all places, like prisoners of war...left to die, all but forgotten, on some desolate rock somewhere in the Pacific. He placed his chances of being found before spring no more promising. They were totally alone....

Something must've happened to RD she surmised ....pacing back and forth, the ominous silence was driving her nuts. She looked at the player piano but lost all desire to deliberate another symphony. She'd rather let it decompose or let her husband have his way with it, and whittle it away to kindling…the only sounds she sought was the reassuring crackling in the massive aperture… The hell roaring hearth. Yet her heart went out to her beloved…there must be something she could do to take his mind off their dire predicament. He energy spent for another go round, she rushed into The chilly culinary crypt, and found the ghetto blaster. The place began to look like a decrepit sector in Harlem or east LA…or some God forsaken war torn zone…during the London blitzkrieg.

She sought some uplifting, timely tune..prayed the boom box still had some battery life left in it…. The hallowed hall burst into a bizarre eerie Emerson, Lake and Palmer tune, blaring….

'and did those feet in ancient time
walk upon England's mountain green
and was the holy lamb of God
on England's pleasant pasture's seen?
And did the countenance divine
Shine forth upon our clouded hills
And was Jerusalem builded here

Upon these dark satanic mills?

The inferences to their dire situation seemed to hit the bulls eye in an uncanny coincidence…as if a demented disc jockey had selected a suitable song, the sum of all their fears realized in the precarious predicament they found themselves in…. There were certainly some sinister forces at play…A reenactment of the wretched industrial revolution. In lieu of child labor or vassals creating the crafty vessels, someone or something had set about to transform the tragedies of their visits into macabre memories only to be cherished by the next novices to set foot in the enchanting premises. A never ending vicious cycle of murder and mayhem…. and only one native American eye witness to retell the tell tale over and over again. As if a privileged or imprisoned participant in a perplexing play, depending on the point of view. A complete turn about that had claimed the lives of all the previous indigenous dwellers on the plain. It was plain as day…as the nose in front of their face…he, now the spectator in the ruthless blood baths that had eliminated both the bison and the innocent bystanders to the slaughter.

Bring me my bow of burning gold

Bring me my arrows of desire

Bring me my spears o clouds unfold

Bring me my chariot of fire.'

(ELP, lyrics –Jerusalem)

Several inferences of Elijah, 2 king 2:11 KJV
ascending to heaven or 2 King 2:17 KJV, urging
the servants to open their eyes to the 'horses and
chariots' of fire that may consume the castle, or
colossal mountain chalet….Dr Gum recalled the
hideous CHAOS card….as he gazed into the
garish…grim ravaged room…as if decimated in a
relentless battle…the forces of good against the
deadly armies of evil…the final battlefield, the
lofty lobby…. Expecting to see RD break down the
door on his trusty steed…and rise up on it's hind
haunches in the middle of the mayhem…He knew
it was all but a fleeting fading frightening dream.
The card could symbolize anything…conformed,
molded, to what ever preconceived nebulous
notion that materialized inside his mind now…
He knew it may still be playing tricks.. over taxed,
underpaid, exactly what the publishers warned as
they whipped the writer into submission. Perhaps it

was them, who had encouraged him to entertain his demons in the deserted residence. He couldn't recall at this moment in time; time the one precious commodity that seemed to slowly slip way…with a fervor, a vigorous vengeance, seeking to find the future, a frightening foreboding finish at some 60 seconds per macabre minute.

> 'I shall not cease from mental fight
>
> nor shall my sword sleep in my hand
>
> till we have built Jerusalem
>
> in England's green and pleasant land'

The lingering lyrics by Emerson, Lake and Palmer inspired by William Blake's poem: 'And Did Those feet in Ancient Time'…left them both spellbound. He took her by the hand to lead her through the promised land…of shattered caviar dreams and champagne wishes…they'd settle for a f…g TV dinner at this juncture.

For a fleeting split second a thought donned on him. Had they indeed felt the presence of Christ? ….walking on the water…dredging the bottom of the icy abyss for the wretched derelicts, the dregs of society? Cleansed of all their sins? An abysmal spine tingling baptism in the icy glacial fed lake?

Like lake Manasaravar, the highest fresh water lake in the world in Tibet (14950') a place of holy pilgrimage like the holy city of Jerusalem? The crazy couple compelled, driven to madness, intent on killing each other..by some evil entity, the devil himself perhaps? lurking in the hallowed haunted halls. Only His omnipotent presence and force, opposing all the obstacles and demons of the occult, the underworld, could ever suffice. He felt his weary overtaxed synaptic connections combined with extreme fatigue created the surreal scenario. The reason for the season? the 4 ghosts? The 4 seasons? Forever announcing the next newcomers destined to pass their short and undoubtedly eventful stay…Then fading away like the falling autumn leaves .. leaving essentially no trace of ever having arrived or accomplished any of the activities on their delightful agenda. And so it seemed that the lovely couple may become another undocumented statistic. There were no records, no ledgers …left. …all the historical facts and data ….consumed in the fire…the figment of his highly over active imagination, the fanciful fonts he found on the philosopher's stone; the alchemists bible?

The book of boundless equations and diagrams to deliver a worthless substance and transform it into precious gold…the very ingredients the greedy chef used to do away with his trusty companion? Were they all inventions of his insidious inherent imagination? That drove him to utter ruin; nearly destitute, destined to die by the demonic devices of his own creation. The manuscript .. in lieu of torching his laptop…the only living testament to their ordeal? Now mere ashes along with all the other previous inhabitants…..

> 'Bring me bows of burning gold
>> bring me my arrows of desire
>> bring me my spears o clouds unfold
>> Bring me my chariots of fire…'

An icy breeze blew in through the ornate balustrade of the upper balconies like a deadly unnerving noxious gas….competing with the warm heated air rising into the upper reaches of the lofty lobby. The turbulent eddies battled like jet fighter pilots in search of a coveted kill to claim the ace card, the emblem emblazond on the bow of the agile predator…like the battle of Britain or search for the bloody Red Baron….

"RD must've gone for help!" he said. He wouldn't be as foolish as they were…defying the elements in the stupid crazy chase… driven to their doom…He'd dressed warm, prepared for the forbidding deep freeze outside unlike the untamed tenants, pursuing their passions with unbridled ambition. He kept chipping away at the concept; slip it into the crevices of his mind as she slipped next to him under cover of their ferocious watch dog. The menacing snarling grimace of the giant grizzly bear….guarded them. by the roaring fire from what? The thin gaunt rug could hardly deter or dissuade a demonic spirit from leaving them alone, any more than their axe or sharp kitchen cleavers could. His weapon of choice? Like the cunning chef…that had committed such heinous atrocities…

Dr Gum turned the page on the persistent images of premeditated murder, preferring to focus his attention on more pleasant thoughts.

"The first national park rangers…" soon engaged in an all encompassing lecture, a rousing stemwinder, the ideal campfire tale in this neck of the woods. "Quite a resilient lot..rode the range

...had to hunt for their food....billions of buffalo roaming"...a bit of Carl Sagan influence?

"Then returned to appease their wives."

"Wives? The pioneers, polygamists?"

"Some of the native practices...."

"Thanks, but no thanks. I was meant for you ...and you alone....we're meant for me!" as she snuggled next to her brave warrior. He'd braved the elements to pursue, likely saved her she realized...The thought of freezing to death in the murky depths slowly sunk in and settled in her conscious. She shuddered, unsettled by the episode. Things seemed to slowly go back to normal? Had all the paranormal activity subsided? Had the demons done all the damage they intended to do? Or was this merely the opening act? The appetizer to their devilishly delicious drama, intent on driving them to cannibalism or other cruel comparably chilling act? She thought it a good time to thaw out and cook whatever RD had killed...before the roaring fire went out. No point letting all the efforts of his endeavors go to waste... or spoil...albeit the slabs of flesh seemed well preserved in the permafrost that began to permeate the prepping stations. She disappeared into the kitchen to see what she'd come up with.

Dr Gum decided to give the RCMP or park wardens another try. The cell phone seemed to be charged, still sitting on the massive dark ebony runway as if forgotten moments prior to departure or deliberately discarded…holding all calls.

Still dead! Damn it! A real dead zone…he didn't like the implications in the statement! As he put down the cell phone…imagining an imminent missed message, perhaps a ring from the premier residing in the Kremlin? intent on relaying rather urgent news assuaging a tense situation… a détente…..he spotted a silhouette dash by outside. The messenger? RD? the harbinger of hope, to deliver a timely transmission. That they'd soon be on their merry way back to the border of civilization somewhere out here on the edge of reason. But as he raced to the back door, he suddenly realized it could be an animal in desperate search of food as they'd soon be. He held his ground anxiously expecting RD to appear. Nothing materialized. His wife turned around stunned by the fixture. The totem pole position was reserved only for RD she chuckled. He'd come around eventually. No need to get his shorts in a knot. Not the thoughts she wanted to dwell on …The frayed ends of St Mary's Cox Comb crept back into her mind…hangman's noose or heaven sent help by the host…It was rather rude of RD not to make an appearance, perhaps a fashionably late entrance in full feathered head dress…she savored the thought in anticipation of an authentic advent to the evening. Accompanied by the spirits of the past, to perform a spirited dance all decked out in decadent Blackfoot décor. The buffalo hides concealing the war wounds and battle scars…the fierce clashes with the white man…as a last resort….summoning the Great Spirit in the sky to answer their desperate plea to fend off the enemy at the gates, against insurmountable odds, in a futile attempt to prevent their very annihilation. An army of ghosts indeed is what they needed to repel the evil entities that remained….or a posse of priests versed in exotic exorcistic exercises to purge the demons of hell that had flocked to the fashionable abode…..an obnoxious black hole sucking all of the dark forces….unto itself and in

so doing dealt a deadly knock out punch
expelling the vital life forces from within…the
final showdown at the OK corral? The extent of
damage and calamity caused this go round seemed
irreparable. The POW would likely succumb
to the sordid shenanigans this time. Their only
hope was to get out while they still could….the
surreal silence seemed like the Alamo…
surrounded on all sides by 5000 blood thirsty
Mexicans waiting just beyond the horizon,
announcing their intents of a clean sweep at
sunrise……

12: Trails

> "Habit is necessary, it is the habit of
> having habits, of turning a trail into
> a rut, that must be incessantly fought
> against if one is to remain alive."
> - Edith Wharton

RD rushed by the large glass expanse at the
back of the hotel leaving a lasting lingering
impression. His broad snowshoes made the going
easy around the buried manicured well maintained
grounds. All but obvious, his tender loving care
and attention to detail removing every scrap of
debris by the amount of snow that had fallen. A
discarded birthday card, or love letter flung from

the fingers of a scorned former mistress, or
lover. Love meant nothing to some of the former
guest, perhaps tennis players? No love lost in some
of the shady clandestine trysts taken. He knew
literally every square inch of the surrounding
countryside… the secret short cuts to the staff
residences…a quick way to the water tower. He'd
covered it countless times. The tall oblong blimp..
reminiscent of an alien UFO attack, it's bulbous
foreboding body on top of the rickety stilts…
preying upon the POW….was frozen, dead in it's
tracks.. the prominent point strategically positioned
to repel any and all foreign advancing armies
…stood it's ground solidly. He couldn't return
empty handed without some hope..or good news
as he slipped by the back door…like the wind.
He'd be back…he figured to bring them good
tidings, to get them on their way to find their future
fortunes. He disappeared behind the massive hedge
that ceased to expand…it's foliage like the
thanksgiving turkey, plucked. Only his prominent
headpiece, a warm raccoon cap, with a bushy tail
trailing behind it…seemed to flit about on the top
of the spiny shrubbery., as if ravaged by a flesh

eating infection….

"An arrow may fly through the air and leave no trace, but an ill thought leaves a trail like a serpent." (Charles Mackay) he thought to himself as he looked back defiantly at the imposing structure. It stood over his shoulder watching him like an abominable snowman, all covered in a foot of snow, that hung from the eaves. Yet by the same token, the vertical apertures, the small alpine window frames also peered down at him…like a million eyes…egging him on…to get the hell off it's property once and for all.

"I'll be back…you hear me?" he yelled…his words lost in the sinuous web of steep valleys and canyons that wove their way through the park… straddling both sides of the world's longest undefended border. How ironic he thought…such an easy escape route.. simply trek through 30 miles of pristine virgin territory from the south side, mind you, it harbored the highest concentration of grizzlies on the planet. An imposing deterrent indeed. The lone sentinel on this side of the boundary stood like a minuteman…albeit not as mobile as the legendary fast deployable forces that warned of the enemies advance during the American Revolutionary war. If only he'd been born on the other side of the tracks, fence or nationality divide. He imagined himself as Paul Revere, the highly revered minuteman, and early warning system. One of the Sons of Liberty … rather than the slaughtered tribes of Blackfoot that roamed the vast wilderness. "There's a long, long trail a winding into the land of my dreams." (Stoddard King) He looked up at the bell tower bewildered and disoriented by it's presence….then took the plunge…much like one of the former staff did.. as they fell into the colorful flower bed one spring. He lost his balance in the snow where he'd turned over the fresh sod only a few short weeks ago. He stumbled, falling to the ground in surreal slow motion…reaching out to brace his fall. He heard a loud snap…not that of a tourist trying to catch a Kodak moment or close up of a Grizzly bear, this image was infinitely more gruesome! The large rotund powerful fangs, rose rapidly from underneath the fresh fallen snow. The razor sharp teeth lined the deadly two foot circumference jaw quickly closed on it's unsuspecting prey. It dug deep as it tore through the thin thinsulate parka. If only he'd been wearing his thick buffalo hide. Practically bulletproof! Such a fool! He was furious yet equally frightened as he peered at the bright red puddle of blood forming around the perimeter of the proboscis. The white canvas was soon covered sporadically in a thick red spray of HIS OWN BLOOD! He panicked, frantically trying to free his arm…he had to find an axe, a sharp implement, his trusty Swiss army knife, to free himself from his unrelenting foe. The force of gravity pulled him to the ground almost into his own blood.. and vomit as he heaved the contents of his delicious cooked fresh venison into the bloody mixture. He frantically tried to yank himself from the chain that held the trap like a dog collar attached to a short leash. It did not let him go, and gave him very little room to roam or maneuver. The damn trap could've brought down a bison or buffalo he figured! All within ear shot and gun sight of an upper floor window. The ghosts, privileged participants in the gruesome spectacle, like rabid fans in the coliseum in Rome cheering for the gladiators…having fed the Christians to the lions.. He had no intention of freezing to death here…although he'd likely bleed to death or pass out from lack of consciousness soon if he didn't resort to something drastic in the few seconds that swiftly flew by. He found his Swiss army knife with his free digits, then with short deep thrusts severed the sleeve and lining to the parka. He dug down to the flesh and found his shoulder locked, pinned down…yet no wrestler in sight. He was in quite a pickle…his only hope he realized was to lop off his arm and limp back into the lobby….the couple could apply a tourniquet .in the nick of time he calculated…but he'd have to hurry. He stabbed repeatedly at the cartilage, and strong tendinous attachments that held his shoulder blade and the upper arm bone in the smooth socket, lock stock and barrel! The pain was unbearable; a sudden surge of endorphins blurred his clarity of thought ….off in the distance he heard the low dull grumble…of…as he raised his head…he caught a brief glimpse of something, shooting a stream of snow and gravel into the side of the highway buried blow a high wall of snow…practically an impenetrable barrier. A huge snowplow? Of course! The reliable road crews making their regular rounds round the remote routes each season!

The driver sat inside the roasty warm glass enclosure of the resilient Zaugg heavy equipment mountain resort plough, like a road warrior. In a daze driven only by the demonic heavy metal tunes tearing his eardrums apart and a faint recollection of where the former narrow slit may have led into the town of Wutherington. The large 10 foot wide swirling set of teeth lapped up the relatively thin snow pack like a row of cocaine with little resistance. The driver was lost in his surreal world, the sound of the grating grinding motion of the revolving teeth, drowned out by the demonic messages emanating from within his head set. Occasionally, a spark startled him, as the steel blades struck a stone, and quickly split it in two; then spit it out with all the other effluent flying from the small chute hanging from the side of the massive menacing chassis. It left a long linear line at the shoulder of the road.. like a distinct runway delineation.

RD had to hurry, the golden opportunity, likely

his last chance to get help. If only he had some fire water to kill the pain! The occupants wallowed in the surplus from the Weeping Willow lounge, wasting it, while he had a not a drop. Burning it as camp stove fuel, kerosene, such a sought after commodity. So close yet so far! The pain was so unbearable, he nearly passed out. With one last swift slice to free his limb, he felt and heard the knife tear through his flesh down to the very bone in a bizarre futile amputation attempt. He could scream, delirious, but refused to alarm his guests…

The Zaugg plow approached the pivotal point in the road, the T intersection with an arm branching off to his left…that snaked up to the POW off in the distance. The driver slowly shifted gears then resumed his mundane care free pace.

RD saw the large Z on the nearest side of the snow plough coming closer. A reassuring sign …the mark of Zorro, here to save the downtrodden, the illegal aliens…He made his final incision, that left his mark…as he dismembered the bloody appendage and left it in the snow. He held the stump in a futile attempt to plug the red river of blood spraying from his gaping wound that seemed to formed a fuse leading from the tinderbox lit only by the sparse firelight that slipped thrrough the icy cracks of the creaky structure. He was terribly woozy, wobbly but refused to fall down as he bull dozed his way down the hill…He was losing copious amounts of blood…that would likely tap him ere he ever reached the rescue mobile.

The Zaugg driver nodded off a few times from the boring mundane tedious route. He shook his head refusing to fall asleep.

RD refused to fall…every breath conceivably his last, the surge of endorphins in his veins propelled him a couple feet and onto the road. As the one armed bandit raised his appendage to flag down the driver, the groggy occupant veered suddenly erratically to his left to avoid a collision with a deer or elk on the road…the ill elk in Running Deer's omen? To fulfill his fateful prophecy? The tale from the crypt at the trailhead?

"The deer or the elk?…I guess I lo…."
He realized his ultimate fate, the final vision that appeared before his eyes…the sharp wide spinning 10 foot wide blades of death, the TEN OF AIRS,

the frantic feeding frenzy by ten rabid buzzards or vultures. It ground the gravel and a garish totem pole in the middle of the road? wondered the stunned driver as he ground the guts of the obstacle to hamburger…the snowshoes transformed instantly into tiny toothpicks which were splattered on the side of the road in the thick red sticky sauce. The disoriented driver stopped the vehicle…and leapt from the cab. He wondered what he'd hit? It barely slowed his advance, the sparse bright red spray suggested he'd hit something small…. perhaps a deer? He stopped to inspect the spectacular 'strawberry snow cone'.

"Naw…" then hurried back into the warmth of his cab and continued unphased by the delay.

Zaugg 1, Running Deer O.

He'd claimed another road kill victim, so many in fact, he was well on his way to attaining the status of 'ace'..in the macabre competition they'd established a few winters ago. He'd file a report later…He had to be more careful next time, then lunged into the steaming Mcdee's hamburger and fries piled into the Styrofoam carton in the passenger seat. He didn't want it to get cold. The thought crossed his mind; it might've even been a human victim, then shrugged it off. The Zaugg made mince meat out of it anyway, then took another bite of his juicy hamburger patty.

A ghostly apparition smirking from an upper story window satisfied with the results of the horrific hair raising encounter…vanished.

Roxy's bladder pressed down compelling her to get up….

"I have to take a tea pea…."

She grabbed the terry cloth robe and wrapped it around her body snugly.

"I'll keep the wig warm warm" chuckled her wayward wanderer. Roxy sprang to the staircase like an agile young doe then disappeared into the ramparts. He threw a few more severed slivers from the Macabre renovation onto the flames…as she reached a first floor room, forsaking the flight of stairs into the dark decrepit dungeon, she checked the icy door knob…Roxy hadn't noticed the sinister scratched message scrawled in the remainder of the woodwork….the fragments spelled:

K I L L ..R

From any one of the upper balconies. But her bladder demanded her utmost attention as she rushed like a race horse to the ensuite toilet. She spread her robe, then sat on her throne pushing the posh permafrost laiden curtain aside to stare off into the vast desolate landscape then screamed.

A river of blood ran through the parking lot...the sinuous trail snaked all the way to the turn off. The source of the unsightly red rivulet, a mystery to her...it seemed to run from the front the POW itself.

"Must be imagining things....again!"

She relieved herself...and closed her eyes, then stood up...She opened them, but found the red river remained...running from the actual hotel itself....she had to get out of there ASAP, before it drove her mad! Claiming another victim, ready to be committed!

From a distance, her ghostly gaunt grimace.... consumed but one of the small Swiss chalet frames as per the previous apparition. The silence did not convey the screaming at the top of her lungs inside of the suite. She let the curtain close....the final curtain call?

As she ran from the room, she paused to indeed discover the odd arrangement of fragments of fine furniture. In a daze she...had difficulty deciphering the deadly message...but was certain It spelled....

K I L L

...then spotted the R... ridiculous!

She screamed again as the lone arranger returned from the bar....on another bender? Several bottles tucked under his arms....He saw her standing there, momentarily flustered, figuring it was but a figment of his imagination, perhaps another feisty ghost keeping an eye on their progressive descent into madness?

"The cost of heating this place is driving me to drink" he repeated himself...not that he recalled, and bent down to douse the flames, lap up the expensive lighter fluid...the flames burst and soon filled much of the hearth. She was shivering from the drafty balcony, wondering whether he'd quit cold turkey...eliminating the cravings of the intoxicating elixir of life, or whether he was up to his old tricks again. He watched him empty several bottles. Satisfied she dared to descend the stairs

…rather than freeze to death. He flung several shards with a fever pitch into the back of the heaping mound of embers and ash building in the blast furnace, afraid they'd never get out before spring training season returned…perhaps never! Disillusioned he sat there desperately trying to keep up with the rapid heat loss. She returned to the middle of the forsaken foyer…as if coming across a forlorn lost soul in the wilderness. In a daze in the aftermath of a fatal wreckage or simply eeking out a meager existence as homeless vagrants in the vast ruins of dilapidated public housing in Harlem…the regal residence returning to it's rightful owners, the hands of the people ..merely the powerless pawns in this perplexing play. They sensed it was slowly drawing to a grand finale. The hotel….had snared them, captured them, closing in on them, their claustrophobia came back…as they sat there now confined to the proximity of the blazing blast furnace. They watched in terror…awaiting their fate….as the flames danced higher…the draft continued to suck a steady stream of particulate matter from the main chimney like a massive liposuction procedure….it seemed to be sucking the very life, the very bone marrow out of the two shivering, shaking occupants......

"Who knows where things will end once they begin?" (Hillcrest – the character in John Galworthy's Skin Game, Nobel prize recipient for Literature) wondered Roxy, grateful to still be alive.... by the skin of her teeth.

They grew very sleepy due to their ordeal and slowly slipped into sweet slumber...in each other's arms. The roaring fire crackled and danced in front of them ...seeming to summon the spirits of former generations of native dancers...yet not a one was to be found anywhere...

13: Smoke Signals

"You know there are some children who aren't really children at all, they are just pillars of flame that burn everything they touch. And there are some children who are just pillars of ash, that fall apart when you touch them…Victor and me, we were children of flame and ash."
-Smoke Signals 1998

The prominent persistent puffs of smoke rising from the general vicinity town of Wutherington alarmed the local authorities…The local park rangers knew that everyone had uprooted and left just prior to the expected cold snap. It was such a bitter early onset of winter this year, that even the most resilient diehards had gone south for the winter.

The two seasoned veterans sat staring off into space stunned by the sight that cast a dark cloud like a foreboding omen over the townsite. Even from the other end of the 8 mile long frozen snow covered lake, the plume was clearly visible. The ranger station at 'Ghost Haunt' sat on the shore at the edge of a vast green velvet carpet that reached up into the tall timber lined terrain now completely buried, covered in a heavy white blanket of snow.

"The Chinese army used smoke signals to alert adjacent towers as far away as 300 miles (500km) along the Great Wall of China ….as did native tribes to warn of white man's advance into their territory."

His long time partner, the pretty model type… A rather deceptive exterior…alleviating all the mystique of the rugged outdoorsy stereotype, raised her binoculars…to focus on the source of the smoke.

"Someone's smokin' a mighty big peace pipe." She assumed it could even be the local yokels camped out in the hotel again…with a particularly large stash of 'medicinal marijuana'… As they preferred to describe it…to kill the pain, perhaps from breaking a limb, caught by surprise falling from a treacherous part of a trail…

"You figure? …as he reached for the ocular apparatus wrapped around her neck. "No one stays in Wutherington, over the winter other than a couple hardy die hards. The POW's boarded up for 9 months of the year. Even the 'Stairway to Heaven' highway is only open 2-3 months contingent upon inclemental weather. Sometimes 15-30' of snow fall at the summit of the Great Divide…"

"So, who do you suppose is out there?" she questioned, getting a queasy feeling in the pit of her stomach. The thought of venturing across the vast frozen wasteland did not sit well with her.

"Those damn ghost chasers. The paranormals pokin' about again?!" He tries the radio….the ham, all emergency frequencies…fiddling with the dials…nothing but dead silence.

"That's weird" she stated.

"Might have to check it out…take the skidoo out

for a spin." Cabin fever had crept into his circulatory system. He needed an excuse, and in lieu of a dog to take for a regular run, he bundled up to take the ski-dog as they were initially intended to be labeled, for a run.

He pointed to a large 3D map model of the 'Peace Park'...Wutherington Lake straddled the US - CDN border...4 miles on the American side, 4 miles on the other side of the border. The lone outpost at Ghost Haunt, was the only 'sane' means to cross into Canada through the menacing mountainous terrain. Many a lost soul had succumbed to the natural elements including a particularly large number of indigenous residents, namely the grizzly bears, the highest concentration in the world. The guardians, a deadlier deterrent than security guards at a maximum security prison; albeit this refuge one had no perimeter fencing.

The initial park rangers and native residents seemed to survive, in fact made a comfortable coexistence...covering the entire park in a day on horseback, blazing trails, wrestling buffalo, returning to their numerous wives, then got up and did it all over again from day break to sunset.

A hardier lot than today. In fact reminiscent of the resilient albeit ill fated explorers of other equally harsh environments. Scott of the Antarctic came to mind. The ranger realized they were only about the same distance Scott reached from 'One Ton Depot' on his fateful last trip. His 'last entry. For God's sakes look after our people.' (Mar 29, 1912). The eerie lingering request..a double edged sword for it may have referred to the local native population that slowly insidiously disappeared at the hands of the white man.

He felt confident the frozen surface could easily support a snowmobile. He'd beeline straight for the border, then bolt to the south west corner of Wutherington, toward the RCMP station, then blaze a trail up to the POW. He suspected it was the source of the large smoke screen. Lurking in the back of his mind was the thought of having to brave a blinding blisteringly cold white out. The breezes ripped through the valleys unannounced He knew the sub zero temperatures could kill in minutes anyone caught unawares by surprise.

The ranger, nearing retirement, stepped outside and prepared his workhorse, the Expedition Rev

XU, with winch, ER sleds, flares, medical supplies…and food. If only Scott had had this vital resilient piece of equipment rather than the 34 dogs and 24 horses purchased in Siberia, transported to New Zealand, the nearest point of departure. They all soon succumbed to the bitter cold, chopped up for horse meat hamburgers….

**

The disgruntled drunk driver…stepped from his idling death machine, still in shock. The Zaugg purred ready for more. He rushed into the maintenance facility that sat at the very perimeter of the park

"Damn, I must've hit a moose"..he estimated by the size of the antler, why it had lost the other one was anyone's guess. The creature's ghastly grimace, he swore it seemed so life like…even 'human'. "…near the Wutherington turn off…left a bloody mess."

The other drivers were sharing some festive spirits, and did not notice the booze on his breath. They offered him a stiff drink to take his mind off the accident.

"Well ace…all in a day's work. Get over it. No

guts…no glory" they chuckled. Then took a
stiff swig from the half empty bottle of JD.
"You've got a week off coming up, why don't you
get away?"

"Yeah, guess you're right…but you know…
there's one thing botherin' me…the look on that
animal's face…freaked me out. Only had one
antler…" realized it must've been in considerable
pain…likely did it a favor, and put it out of it's
misery.

"Aw get over it, it was over in a flash!"

"If it makes you feel any better, I'll check the
route for any injured critters on my next run…"
The crew occasionally found a shaking, shivering
creature by the roadside, that continued to cull and
thin the herds…

"Thanks."
**

The hotel will still be here long, long, after you're
gone! thought Roxy as ghastly groans emanated
deep from within her groins under the warm fur
from the gutted victims.

They stirred as the fire was losing it's luster and
soothing warmth. The author, aware of the dire

situation sprang to the bar to order a few more rounds. He'd run up quite a tab...the likes of which the POW had never seen by two stranded politically incorrect campers. They'd gutted the place, nearly burned down the house, and still seemingly not purged their demons from the dwelling. He must've known his number was nearly up...as he proceeded to pour more potent offerings onto the fire. He realized they were running out of wood then turned his attention to the old player piano. He preferred the sounds of silence to his deceptive prodigy's decadent display of affection as she so lovingly stroked the ivories... earlier. Her place was in the kitchen to cook him up some grub he felt, not fingering the keys ...eliciting the macabre enchanting melody. Determined to put the player piano out of it's misery he began to compose a tune of his own. The sound of the splintered aging wood, laced with whiskey and taut wires emitted a few eerie sounds as if severing a cat...or other shrieking helpless little furry creature. He attacked the relic with no remorse and complete abandon...as if destroying the devil himself....

Roxy shivered n front of the frosty ice box. Decadent frozen TV dinner like entrails, their frozen drops of blood in suspended animation, …hung from the glass shelves.

"Too much blood" she shook her head in disbelief.

"The beginnings and endings of all human undertakings are untidy" (John Galsworthy, Nobel Prize in literature 1932.) ruminated in her mind. Famished she had to get food into her gut and fast!

Still wielding the axe, he stumbled into the kitchen….

"Let me give you a hand…" He raised the axe. It worried her…bleary eyed, his aim may not be true or what it used to be. The hand he was referring to may very well be her own, if she didn't get out of the way while she still could. The axe struck the open vault. It severed several frozen strips of flesh and fresh venison that dispersed and slid on the frozen surface like boulders ….alongside the ovens like a rock hurled in a bonspiel.

"Thought we'd stir up some pot luck" as he tossed the pieces into a large cauldron…with a stark raving mad look. She feared she'd be next on the menu…and motioned for the back door. He found some cans of pork and beans and in lieu of a can opener aligned the cans on the counter like a crazed executioner then quickly lopped the lids off the hard head tin containers…and tossed them into the pot….Several minutes passed before he noticed the oven was not on….staring at the pot, expecting a simmering stew. Instead the frozen chunks…congealed..and stuck together…as if cowering about to be boiled alive in a cannibalistic tribal ritual…somewhere in the South Seas….

She dashed from the kitchen.. and raced to the fire…desperately seeking a weapon in her defense. She grabbed one of a giant pokers preparing a duel to the death. Poised…panic stricken she grabbed the dull heavy implement with both hands…then stood her ground backing toward the roaring fire. She dared not retreat nor take another step back …the result? spontaneous combustion…She shivered, crying…not knowing what had come over him..as he dragged the heavy sleigh of sloppy entrails and dragged it toward the fire. The sight of her standing there…suddenly inspired him and gave him a brilliant idea. He dropped the axe….

and requested she turn over the poker. She
reluctantly complied....wondering what the cause
of his complete about face was.

He resourcefully grabbed the other long
implements and placed them quickly in the dying
embers and formed a makeshift tripod from which
to hang a pot, luckily just in the nick of time.

He ran and grabbed another row of bottles
..having preferred to taste the sweet elixir, the
water of life, now the only source of cooking or
heating their concoction.

The determined dentist fished through the
cauldron as if selecting the lucky ticket holders
number..in a Gordo multi million dollar lottery
then picked the empty cans out one by one
...leaving only the sloppy mixture which slowly
began to melt and simmer to a boil.

She still dared not approach the bubbling
cauldron for fear that he'd still dunk her head in it
as if bobbing for apples...

"Now giddy up and get me some grub, woman"
he demanded...that they return to their expected
role playing, her the part of the provider, she the
cute camp cook, his concubine.. slaving over a

hot stove as in the days of yore…She returned from the kitchen with a handful of spices…looking like a sooty filthy witch…about to sprinkle some magic dust into the mixture and make the hideous nightmare go away!

"The colonel's secret?" asked the dumbfounded chef.

"Our little secret" she said…then slowly blew the spices in the general direction of the cauldron. The spices ignited in a colorful dazzling pyrotechnic display…only adding to the mystique of the relative lack luster ingredients. A hill of beans… piles of pork percolated in the pot. There'd be enough natural gas or methane generated after their food orgy he assumed. Likely enough to lift the roof off the lobby!

She stirred the stew slowly steadily preserving all the natural juices and fragrant aroma inside, then replaced a large garbage can lid…

"A spoonful of lovin'!"

Simply… "Irresistible" he replied licking his chops…he took a long ladle to sample the mixture. His discriminating taste buds determined…

"Needs a little …splash of…liquor" as he licked

the ladle…leering at his sous chef, saving her for dessert.

"The fiesta resistance? In our opulent…." As she peered around the ruins.. she rephrased the ending, "poor man's party." She prepared a heapin' helpin' of lovin'.

"Let's take if from the top, this time no 'death by chocolate'." They devoured the decadent slapped together surprisingly delicious dish. Spooning each other in front of the roaring fire.

"You only live once, but if you live life right, once is enough."

"Once is never enough… with a girl like you."

They shared each other's dessert, then delved in to decadent passionate foreplay…after a few rounds, they passed out by the fire.

**

The resilient Ghost Haunt ranger reached the border. The bitter north winds and blinding snow made the rest of the trek impossible. Like an invisible impenetrable barrier, they could not approach the tiny town, trapped in a treacherous white out.

They returned to the Ghost Haunt station empty

handed, and dejected. The elder ranger rushed to get the word out.. to anyone in their neck of the woods to . 'for God's sakes, get to the POW!'

"Still no contact with the outside world. We'll just have to ride her out."

**

The open lid that had seemingly sucked the life blood out of the hotel, and all the toxic fumes with it, had slammed shut. The life saving stack effect failed as the clogged flue…practically sealed their fate. The dense toxic clouds of carbon monoxide filled the foyer and rose in the lofty lobby, obscuring the captive audience, a few apparitions that had stayed to the bitter tragic end of the final fateful performance. A heavy cloud descended and hung over the decrepit stage, as if to parody the final curtain call..

**

"Better make my rounds" said the maintenance crew. "I don't like the looks of that rising plume.

"The native's restless? Must be some POW WOW!"

"Goin' after griz by the look of it" surmised the seasoned staff member. Only the hardiest trapper or hunter would venture these treacherous conditions.

"I'll bring out the big guns!"

Loaded for bear, the big Tucker rig could handle the toughest inclemental weather conditions. Independent 4 tread traction…plenty of pulling power…they'd reach the POW come hell or high water!

The snow cat finally turned over…the sluggish diesel ground through the transmission….slowly idling at a steady purr. They loaded the cab with survival gear, ER kits, filling the small brandy kegs, they strapped the lifesaver around the eager Extra.

"Ata boy Berry" as he scratched his neck. The feisty friendly St Bernard lapped his face…the eager beaver back seat driver…leapt around the pilot's seat panting heavily.

"Let's go find 'em!"

The powerful Tucker 1644 'Fire Slip In Unit' specially outfitted for fire control, SAR, winches blazed a trail through the wilderness, and beelined for the POW, the most prominent standing landmark in sight. Everything else was buries under a sea of snow and ice.

They arrived in the nick of time…smoke belched from each window of the huffy haunted hotel as if about to explode. They opened the door.

Berry dashed to the front door, pawing frantically to get inside, like some crazed bear marking his territory. The rest of the crew in full gear soon followed.

**

Dr Gum squinted in the midst of the nebulous, nauseous concoction of fumes….finding his bearings…from the foreboding desolate landscape that lay outside the dangling double front doors…. an icy breeze shot through him like a cold steel saber to his very soul….. The pain awoke him…the picture indelibly etched in his conscious. What permanent damage that may have marred his and his bashful bride's subconscious …was any one's guess….several ghostly silhouettes sauntered through the stark smoky entryway….

"You're searching for something that doesn't exist. Ends and beginnings….there are no such things." (Robert Frost, poet) He wondered if the words ever left his frost bitten lips. As futile an attempt as finding any sign of life….or evidence of any lingering ghostly guests…..Lost in the desperate search and rescue attempt to extract any unfortunate souls, a firefighter …stopped briefly.

"You say something?"

"If you must smoke take your butt outside!" ribbed his partner in crime…

"It's easy to quit smoking, I ought to know, because I've done it a thousand times." (Mark Twain, American humorist), ha, ha."

The words were lost amongst the sooty smoke and debris that rose up into the lofty obscured lobby….yet the words seemed to resonate with the disoriented dentist….How many victims had succumbed to the sinister shenanigans conducted at the seemingly serene retreat over the decades? How many more unwary travelers would venture through it's unassuming entrance and enter into the surreal chilling recurring nightmare?…over and over….for all eternity? Until the aging structure finally collapsed…imploded upon itself? Taking it's sinister secrets with it? Or was there something more demonic at work here? Did the evil entity set it's sights specifically on these two lovebirds. Two lost souls who happened to venture into the luxurious lair?....taunting them, testing their faith? The very foundations of their cherished Judaeo Christian beliefs? The questions buzzed about in his head in an endless clanging...a macabre merry go round....He held his ears....

He tried to imagine infinity....a never ending circle...round and round....Roxy, his delightful damsel in distress caught his attention out of the corner of his eye...Everything seemed to fade.... out of focus. He knew he'd spend the rest of time with her....no matter what may come their way.

"Oh Bernard, a little lower..." she cooed as a large slobbery tongue consumed her face..She awoke clutching the wears of a ...rabid dog? Then leapt up...

"Your ears bitten to?" questioned Roxy weakly... wondering what the long term toll on the two of them might be.. She could not feel her legs...still scared stiff she supposed....recalling a few tales from undertakers who had taken up residence in some of the quaint century old cabins lining the perimeter of Enchanted Bay... she shuddered...

Lucky she had survived the ordeal and not
ended up on the slab in their lab....

"Did you hear the one about the undertaker's
daughter? Where the thoughts came from she knew
not! "He buried more stiffs than she did!"...
"Remember if you're smoking after sex, you're
doing it too fast."...resonated in her head....she let
out a hideous haunting bellow....of a laugh.... Her
hot, heavy flammable expulsion sent a shock wave
through the smoky frosty air It seemed to stir them
all back to their senses ...The senselessness of it
all...Roxy shook her head dusting the sooty debris
from her disheveled hair... and slowly crawled
toward the door. She had to get out NOW. The wet
walls doused in a precautionary foam....moved,
and seemed to close in around her....an acute case
of claustrophobia set in ...choking her strangling
her...this was not an aversion to the jolly old St
Nick (Claustrophobia- Fear of Santa Claus?) but a
full blown breathing impairment ....pulmonary
pressure...as if an evil entity were trying to mount
her...and squeeze the last breath of life from
her....Roxy clawed her way to the entrance like a
caged animal...coming from its sanctuary, it's

enclosure at the first sign of spring…inching her way along the decrepit charred foam covered hardwood floors…A firefighter grabbed her…

"Come on, let's get you two outta here!

He looked at her forlorn face. A chill came over him as he caught a glimpse of something so evil deep in her haunting hazel eyes….He shook.. stunned….

"You must've been through some nightmare" he said.. "Come on Joe, give me a hand., hurry."

"Sure thing…" The resourceful rookie ran over and grabbed her delicately….the two dragged her onto another warm blanket…sandwiched her with an equally soothing layer of synthetic fabric..then gently hoisted her onto a stretcher….

She peered back anxiously into the depths of the dreary diorama….the venomous veil was slowly dissipating.. beyond the endless ghostly pale panorama….of permafrost and snow…. She knew not whence she came nor where she was going but she felt she had to get the hell out of there ASAP! It gnawed at her guts…. She left the lobby….to rejoin the lively chatter amongst the land of the living…. Her stomach ached….begging for food…for nourishment….A sickly queasiness enveloped her….as she turned her head about to vomit….the bloody grim reminders of Running Deer's desperate failed attempt to fetch help came into focus. The anticipated appearance of new fresh falling snow to mitigate the garish gruesome scene was no where to be found. In stead the sinuous trail and stench and of the red rivulet lingered….then disappeared in the distance under the snow plough's tracks….She heaved what little fluid and fragments of former 'decadent desserts' that remained in the pit of her stomach. It caught the young firefighter quite unawares…His foot wear was doused in colorful chunks of partially digested debris blending into a bloody, slimy soup… that trickled under the vehicle…. The wretched stench seemed to spur them on….igniting their intents to get out fast. The couple was hustled out of harm's way in the event of an explosion, the lingering odor of toxic fumes and effluent was everywhere. The fire crew hurried them into the warm roasty toasty Tucker Snow cat. The 1644 Fire Slip Unit In Unit blasted out a soothing stream of heat. Berry, by their side, barked and pawed them persistently to insure they not nod off…and slip into unconsciousness. His relative, and European counterpart had saved anywhere from 40 to 100 souls in the Swiss Alps due to exposure to the elements. Their ordeal inside the haunted halls no less horrifying than a stranded trapper lost in this hellish neck of the woods.

The captain cleared the building, satisfied there were no other survivors lying about…
Dr Gum and Roxy looked at each other; both spotted the ghostly silhouette in the upper reaches of the structure…certain of it's permanent residency…in the aging accommodations…that had served as an icy asylum for the past …they couldn't believe how many weeks had passed …since their arrival. Roxy counted them on her frozen fingertips. They were all there…

The panting bartender, Berry, was eager to oblige, as the captain reached around the animal's neck to loosen his collar…an allow him to pour a few stiff shots of Courvoisier XO, from his keg. The extra old, aged for some 20 years, blend certainly hit the spot. Roxy greedily slugged it back, having acquired a taste for every imaginable alcoholic beverage and activity during their brief 'honeymoon'. Their only souvenir, an embroidered POW terry cloth robe. The laptop was never found, perhaps it was best to let sleeping dogs lie reasoned the author. They peered up into the ramparts and wondered when the next weary lost souls would set foot inside. Hopefully never. The place should've been condemned, burned to the ground, to drive the demons or whatever evil entity that lurked inside, out....forever. But alas, such is the case of historic landmarks, closely guarding their sinister coveted sordid dirty little secrets...that lay buried deep inside...

The captain poured another bloody red mixture of Courvoisier,

"A Borodino Berry, in honor of our lovable mascot." A real life saver, indeed...discovering their lifeless bodies.. dragged from the hearth. The special blend of 4 mashed berries, perhaps in honor of the 4 ghosts of the POW the only other survivors of the hellish ordeal. 15 ml of Chambord, 50 ml of Courvoisier exclusive, XO, lemon juice, a dash of soda, vanilla sugar....Not as bitter a pill to swallow as the painful prescription for disaster that they had endured.

"Bottom's up!" declared Dr Gum. Roxy mimicked his gesture and let the soothing elixir of life flow though her insides...

EPILOGUE

 The sinister presence, the prominent permanent
fixture nestled atop the mountain mesa, had
claimed another victim, in it's relentless quest for
blood. Yet two untimely travelers had miraculously
eluded it's deadly jaws of death, seemingly just in
the nick of time. Their ordeal indelibly etched into
their minds, likely forever. Rather than a fond
memory, now a recurring nightmare. Destined to
question their sanity and sense of self in the
senseless display of debauchery and butchery that
took place inside. Driven to the depths of human
depravity, the intoxicating creature comforts they
craved so much, ultimately almost did them in, in
the God forsaken regal residence. Dare they ever
venture back inside the hallowed haunted halls? Or
simply close the books on the chilling chapter of
their lives? They knew one fact, the irrevocable
calamity was bound to recur as the next tourist
season rapidly approached. The POW's, regal
façade, fully restored to it's former feisty splendor
commanded an air of respect from each passerby.
Everyone marveled the wonderful architectural

monument sitting silently, deceptively waiting to prey upon the next victim, nare a weary wanderer that wasn't drawn inside, if only to satisfy a morbid piqued curiosity as they came to the sleepy mountain retreat, near the town of Wutherington that lay at the end of the road.

BIBLIOGRAPHY

Haunted Hotels: Ghost Stories from the Prince of Wales Hotel. Freeland, Benjamin. The Boundary, Aug 29, 2008.

High on a Windy Hill: The Story of the Prince of Wales Hotel. Ray Djuf. Rocky Mountain Books. Feb 25th, 2009.

Wreck of the Gertrude: www.Shorediving.com

Emerald Bay, Waterton AB

Kilmorey Lodge burns to the ground. Jan 20th, 2009, Calgary.ctv.ca

Dickens, Charles. Bleak House. 1853 Bradbury and Evans. Spontaneous Combustion. eg. character Krook

Holzer. Hans. Ph.D. The Supernatural: Explaining the Unexplained. New Page Books. 2003
TV series: "In Search of…"

Holzer. Hans. The Ghost Hunter: Chilling Tales of Real Life Hauntings. Barnes and Noble. 2005

Houran and Lange. Hauntings and Poltergeists: Multidisciplinary Perspectives. McFarland & Co. 2001.

Long, Max Freedom. The Secret Science Behind Miracles. Evinity Pub. Apr. 8, 2009.

The author, Bernie Unrau, a dentist by training, stumbled across a four minute video back in 1989, an interview with the prolific Robin Cook, a physician by training. His mastery of the medical thriller inspired Bernie to embark on a 2nd career and a new uncharted course each summer. The central character in his novels, Dr Gum, perhaps part bumbling lieutenant Columbo or the deductive

Sherlock Holmes the imaginary detective
created by Sir Conan Doyle, also a physician; the
tenacity of Dr Ryan conceived by Tom Clancy, or
the curiosity of Indiana Jones A dash of the dapper
James Bond blended in, shaken and stirred into the
equation the inspiration of in depth concept
research of Michael Crichton and his creations or
the powerful suspense of a John Grisham legalistic
thriller. Or to simply bring some of his years as a
dentist, lecturer and inventor to light by engaging
in espionage, elucidating an enigma, disclosing the
dastardly or diabolical scheme, or dreaming up a
formidable frightening future. And as the prolific
Zane Grey, dentist turned novelist turned
screenwriter at the turn of the century, pen 100
books. The author has enjoyed travel, tennis,
sailing, skiing, flying, reading and thinking. He is
single and currently resides in Calgary, Alberta.

Books and Screenplays by Dr Bernie Unrau:

Terra Vista
Deadly Implant
Not A Drop
Golden Mask
Questa
Rook
Hooked
Big B
Enlightened
The Board
The ROM
New Millenium
Reflections
Submarine Slide
Sabotage
Dentinator
Ubar
Stemwinder
Pulling Strings
Meltdown
Pulpit Fiction
Confusion
Glazers
Glazers
God Almighty
The Scrying
Rising

Order from:
www.caltexpress.com
www.publishersgraphicsbookstore.com
Or all major outlets

Screenplays:

Chokepoint
Ultra Stealth: War Game(s)
Phantom of the Operatory
Montauk Monster
Deep Fright
Jabberwhacky
Pandemonium
Deep Fright: Down Under
The Curse of the 7 Pagodas
Sweet Tooth
Cravings
Fantastic Voyage II
The Ice Forest
The Frozen Chosen
Insight
Subterranea
East of Aden
The Glass
The X Files: The Grey Zone